RESENTFUL ROCKSTAR

THE BURNT CLOVERS

GINA AZZI

ONE
ALLEGRA

"THE BURNT CLOVERS have made headlines in every major city in Europe."

I glare at the television screen that hangs in the corner of the bar.

An image of Derek, looking just as sexy as the last time I saw him—he was naked and wrapped in the navy sheets of his bed—splashes on screen. It quickly spins out to an image of my brother, drunk, high, and disoriented. Levi's hair is a mess, sticking out at odd directions, and his eyes are empty. But he's smiling. He's cheesing so hard, his jaw could crack.

"But their tour is coming to an abrupt halt now that rhythm guitarist, famed Levi Rousell, has checked into rehab. We've confirmed reports this morning that Levi..."

Ugh. I sneer and turn away from the television. I don't want to hear any more. I don't want to see images of Derek or Levi or even my friend Mav, blitzed or laughing. Not when the pain of their abandonment, over four months old, hasn't scabbed over.

One of the bartenders, Devy, turns off the television. "Hey, Allegra, you're in section B tonight."

"Okay," I reply, not caring which group of tables I have. While some of the girls complain that one section trumps another, my tips are solid. I know how to joke, interact, and talk to my tables—a giggly bachelorette group or a pack of guys looking to blow off steam—and it pays off in the form of much-needed cash.

I've been serving cocktails at the popular lounge, Beirut, since the start of last semester. Since I returned to LA jaded, heartbroken, and mostly uninterested in things that used to matter.

"You look hot, mama," Luis, one of the bouncers, greets me with a kiss to the temple.

Beirut boasts a solid crew, and I've enjoyed my time working here. But I'm here out of necessity, not for extra spending money. When The Burnt Clovers kicked off their European tour without a backward glance, without so much as a good-bye, I left Boston.

Sure, Mav reached out and offered to rebook my flight after my friend Buck's funeral. Yeah, my brother Levi checked in twice, via text, to see if I wanted to join him in Paris.

But they don't know the full story.

They don't know that Derek Reiner made love to me the night before. That he kissed me soulfully and called me his everything.

No matter what happens, just know that the way I feel for you, it's real.

He fucking lied.

Because not even twelve hours later, he was wheels up on a flight to London and I was sobbing on his bedroom floor wondering what the hell happened.

At first, the band's tour dates filled my every conscious thought. I scoured the internet for photos of the guys; I listened to the radio to hear their songs. But after a few weeks passed and I put the pieces together—Derek lied to the band and said I stayed behind for Buck's funeral—I moved on.

I flew back to LA. I re-enrolled in a few classes at UCLA.

Ivy, Nova, and Kenny already had a three-bedroom apartment and their usual college commitments. Ivy's on the softball team, Kenny's applying to law schools, and Nova's just as boy crazy with a new guy every week.

So, I rented a dingy studio off campus and picked up this gig at Beirut. In my spare time, I continue the type of work that filled my cup this summer in Boston.

I'm working with the homeless in LA. I'm giving back to a community I care about. I'm doing good work that Buck would be proud of.

And Derek Reiner and the rest of the band can fuck right off.

"You ready, girl?" Luis asks, flipping his chin in my direction.

"Yeah." I grin and shake off thoughts of the Clovers.

I'm numb to any news of them now. It doesn't even phase me that my brother's in rehab. Months ago, I'd be sobbing over his downward trajectory. Now? Now, I don't have the emotional bandwidth to worry about anyone else's bullshit.

Now, I'm being me, enjoying my life, and doing work I care about. Full stop.

Luis opens the door and the handfuls of groups waiting outside trickle in. The lights are dim, the music low and sensual, the environment inviting and exciting.

I fiddle with my top, making sure my breasts are concealed but show enough skin to tempt. I rake my fingers through my short hair, fluffing it up at the roots. When the first group of guys takes a seat in my section, I run my tongue over the front of my teeth and grin.

It's showtime.

I sashay to their table, pop my hip, and greet them. "Hey, guys, thanks for coming tonight. I'm Allegra and I'll be taking care of you this evening."

"Hey, Allegra," one of the men replies. "I'm Alex. This is Tommy and Ramon." He points to his friends.

I shoot Alex a wink, watching as his eyes spark. He's good-looking, with dirty blond hair and hazel eyes. He's wearing a black fitted button-down, with the sleeves rolled up on his forearms. Black ink travels up his arms and disappears under the cuffs of his shirt.

I bite my bottom lip, liking what I see. He's got enough of an edge to pique my curiosity, yet his features are in opposition to the man who's ruled my mind for far too long.

Derek's whiskey eyes and unruly, dark hair take up too much space in my head as it is. Wouldn't it be nice to get lost in two pools of hazel rather than drown in bottomless whiskey?

"Can I start you guys off with something to drink?" I ask.

They order a bucket of beers and a round of tequila shots. I nod before stopping by the other two tables that are now brimming with patrons to introduce myself.

Yeah, tonight's going to be a good night. My section is filling up, my tables are solid. And Alex is just the distraction I need to ensure I remain desensitized to all Clovers news.

I'm not wondering about Derek. Or worrying about Levi.

I'm working. And when my shift ends, I'm hitting a party.

———

MY SHIFT PASSES QUICKLY with Alex and his friends at one of my tables.

"Take a shot with us, Allegra!" Ramon hollers when I pass by a few hours later.

I laugh and shake my head, noting how Alex's eyes drink in my curves. He doesn't disguise his interest and I revel in it. The attention, the desire, the reassurance that I'm not totally damaged. Just slightly bruised.

I sidle over to their table. "You really want another round?"

Ramon grins and Alex chuckles.

"Only if you're drinking with us," Alex says.

I give a little nod. While we're not supposed to get blitzed during our shifts, our manager is pretty laid-back. Each server has a $100/shift cap to purchase drinks in case it's someone's birthday or a friend pops by. We're also allowed to take a shot or two if we can handle it.

If the past few months have taught me anything, it's that I can handle my liquor.

"I'll be right back," I tell the guys.

I hear Tommy snicker and Alex cheer in the background.

I step to the server's station.

"What do you need?" Devy asks.

"Four tequila shots," I say, adding the order to my portable POS system.

Devy glances at the table of guys and her eyes narrow. "For table two?"

"Yeah," I confirm.

She looks at me, her gaze studying. "Be careful with them, Allegra. I know Tommy from years ago and they're a wild bunch. Good guys but they party really hard."

I nod, pasting a smile on my face. "Thanks, Devy," I say, wanting to reassure her.

A thrill shimmies down my spine and my stomach clenches in anticipation. Tonight, I want to party hard. I want to shake off the shitty thoughts that whisper on the edges of my mind about Levi and the band.

Since I heard the news earlier, I've had to work to push away thoughts of Derek. And here I thought I was healing, icing him out, numbing myself to the pain.

I shoot Devy a grin as she places four shot glasses on my tray.

I slow my gait and make sure Alex's eyes are on mine as I approach his table. I pass out the shot glasses and tuck the small round tray underneath my arm while holding the fourth shot.

I raise it. "Cheers, boys."

Ramon snorts. Alex grins, slow and sexy, like he knows I'm down to fuck. Like he knows how badly I want to turn off my mind and just feel. Something, anything, that isn't painful.

"To you." Alex tilts his glass in my direction.

I lift an eyebrow and toss back the tequila. It goes down easy, just like water these days.

"What time are you finished tonight?" Ramon asks.

"Off at three," I reply, cocking my head.

Alex smirks. "I'll wait for you."

"Good," I confirm.

After that, I leave the boys to their own conversation. I work my tables, do my rounds, banter and smile and engage.

When Beirut closes, I cash out, stash my tips, and say good night to Devy and Luis and the others.

Then, I exit the lounge and note Alex, leaning against a black Mercedes S-class in the middle of the parking lot.

"Where are your friends?" I ask as I approach his ride.

"Waiting for us," he says cryptically.

I shrug and slide into his car.

As he maneuvers out of the parking lot, I pull in a deep breath. His car smells masculine, like cologne and pine. It's clean and comfortable and I let my mind rest as I lean my head back.

"You want to get into fun or trouble?" Alex asks, reaching over to palm my thigh.

His hand slips over my slick, leather leggings, and an image flares to life in my mind.

Wearing these leggings as I approached a Boston brownstone. Knocking on the front door. *His* voice, his eyes, his surprise when he saw me. *Stellina.*

I shake my head to clear it and turn my attention to Alex. I'm here with Alex. "Aren't they the same thing?"

He chuckles and squeezes my thigh in agreement. Minutes later, Alex parks and takes my hand as we walk into a gorgeous, oceanfront property, where the music is bumping, the liquor is flowing, and the pills are popping.

"Glad you came, Allegra," Alex says, and he sounds like he means it.

I grin up at him. "Yeah, me too."

Then, I enter the party, accept the first glass of bubbly pressed into my hand, and hug Tommy and Ramon hello like I haven't seen them in ages, like they're my long-lost friends, and not guys I served an hour ago.

They sweep me into their group. Everyone at the party is animated and fun, sharing exciting stories and discussing various topics. I flit from one group to the next, casting off any self-consciousness and letting the energy of the crowd buoy me up after months of sinking.

It's loud and light. It's a whirlwind I want to sweep me off my feet.

"You good?" Alex asks. He comes up beside me and his fingers press into the small of my back.

I smile up at him, pausing as two of him swim before me. I blink, focus, and—there he is. "I'm great!" I gush. I don't know how many drinks I tossed back, but the last two have certainly pushed me over the edge.

I don't care. Tonight, I want to live dangerously. Recklessly. For the moment. And this is such a beautiful moment.

"I'm glad," Alex murmurs. His hand flattens in the center of my back, slides down and rests on the swell of my ass.

I tilt into his side, eager for his warmth. Connection.

We hang around for a few more minutes and I listen as Alex asks a few questions to the group I was chatting with before he appeared. Then, he takes my hand and leads me up a winding staircase.

I go willingly, giggling when my toe catches on a step.

"Careful, love," he warns.

Love. Derek called me that a time or two. It used to mean something different when he said it. There was a weight to his word, a significance in his tone.

It doesn't matter now.

We clear the steps and Alex guides me into a bedroom. The balcony door is open and the sound of the sea— churning waves and restless water—washes over me. I turn in his arms and lift my chin, ready to meet his kiss.

He dips down and presses his mouth to mine. Hard, firm, and the distraction I've sought all evening.

Our restraint breaks free. The sly glances and quips of the night dissolve in hot, tracking hands and needy, panting breaths. I reach for Alex's pants as he pulls off my shirt. Our clothes form a puddle on the floor. He quickly rolls on a condom.

Clashing teeth, clumsy movements, and then—"Right there," I pant. He enters me on a sharp thrust, pinning my back between the bedroom wall and his hard body.

He fucks me with intention. The need to get off, the desire for release claws up the back of my throat, and I sink my nails into Alex's shoulders. He's relentless and it's just what I need. Angry and edgy and filled with delicious friction.

"Fuck, you feel good," he murmurs. His fingers sink into my ass and grip hard enough to bruise.

I grind against him, throwing my head back. "More."

"Got you," he promises, working me to the edge. "Get there, babe. Get there."

I do. I come hard, swearing at him, as he continues to thrust.

"Fuck," he groans as he reaches his peak.

When he stills inside of me, the scent of our desperation colors the air. Our skin is sticky, our breathing uneven.

I feel him slowly soften inside me before he pulls out and gently places me on my feet.

"You good?" he asks, much like he did twenty minutes out.

"Great," I exhale, trying to regulate my breathing.

Alex nods and disappears into the bathroom.

The breeze ripples over my heated skin, causing a flash

of goosebumps to break out along my arms, down the center of my stomach.

I dress quickly, fixing my top to make sure I'm not flashing too much.

Alex reemerges. "You want a ride back to your car?" he offers.

"Sure," I say casually.

There aren't two of him anymore, but I'm not sober enough to drive. Is he? I shrug. I'm ready to go. I got what I came for and now, I'm tired. Spent. Wanting to be on my own after too much stimulation, too much connectedness.

I find my phone in my purse and consider messaging the girls or calling Nova for a ride.

But I don't want to hear the concern in her tone or explain that I had a perfectly good one-night fuck with a guy whose last name I don't know. Not that Nova would judge. In the morning light, I would.

Or at least, I used to.

Instead, I follow Alex back down the stairs and out to his car. He drives me back to Beirut and drops me off. I stumble through the parking lot, around the side of the building to where I parked.

When I get there, I brace a palm against the side of my car and hunch forward.

The evening churns in my mind. The alcohol burns the lining of my stomach. Acid and regret. Fuck.

My hands grow clammy, and the skin on the back of my neck tightens. I dip farther forward, just as a stream of vomit pours from my throat.

I groan, knowing I should care more about the splatters that kick up and dot along my shoes.

"Gross," I scold myself.

I roll toward my car, dropping my head along my forearm. Take a deep breath in, a slow exhale out.

Images of Derek flicker through my mind. I still taste his kiss. Recall the weight of his body against mine. Remember his words, his voice, the vulnerability in his gaze, when he entered me.

Lies. All fucking lies.

"Hey, you're okay," a voice says right before a heavy hand lands on my shoulder. "Can't drive like this."

The hand shakes me gently and I manage to drag my head up. Force my eyes open.

Whiskey eyes swim before mine.

"Need to sober you up," the man says, leading me toward Beirut. He pulls open the back door and eases me into a chair at the bar.

I slump over. My eyes close on their own accord.

A thump rattles me awake.

"Drink it," the man demands, nudging a glass of water closer. "I put on a pot of coffee."

"I, um, yeah. Thanks," I stammer. I reach for the cool water and take a few gulps. It makes me more alert, and when I set the glass down, I turn my attention toward the stranger. He looks vaguely familiar.

"You work for me?" he asks.

Ah. "You're Dex?" I guess, naming the elusive owner Devy told me about.

"Guilty." He holds out a hand and I shake it.

"I'm Allegra." My cheeks blaze with embarrassment. I can only guess at what Dex is thinking. Shit. I wince. Is he going to fire me?

"Cocktail server?"

I nod.

"You make this a habit?" His flips his chin in my direction.

"Not usually," I admit.

"Bad night?"

"Bad quarter," I answer honestly.

The corner of his mouth twitches, but his eyes darken with concern. "You want to keep working here, you can't get fucked up and drive home."

"I know."

He pours me a cup of coffee. We sit in an easy silence while I sip it.

"I'm going to give you a ride. You can come get your car tomorrow. And then, when you're sober, we're going to talk." He swipes his keys off the bar and gestures for me to slip off the stool.

I follow him out to his ride. A swell of déjà vu, from hours earlier, envelops me. It's like I'm retracing my steps. Going through the motions with no destination, no end goal, in mind.

"Are you going to fire me?" I ask, my voice cracking. I really need this job; I need the money.

"Not yet," Dex mutters, pulling out of the parking lot. "Tell me how to get to your place."

I do.

We make the drive in silence, and when we pull in front of my tiny studio in a run-down part of town, Dex lifts an eyebrow. "Tomorrow. Come in around noon. We're gonna talk."

"Okay," I agree, feeling adequately scolded. Even though Dex has been decent, kind even, the look he turns my way reminds me of my dad. Stern and firm and serious.

"You don't show, you're out of a job."

"I'll be there," I promise.

Dex nods once and I slide from his SUV.

He waits until I'm inside before pulling away, and the action soothes something deep inside me.

Maybe there are still good men. Guys who truly care.

Maybe I'm just not meant for them.

My dad taught me that. Levi solidified it. And Derek? Derek shattered whatever semblance of hope I had left.

I'M hungover and embarrassed when I shuffle into Beirut the following day.

"Morning," Dex greets me.

I lift a hand to wave.

He tilts his head toward the back. "Let's go to my office. Talk."

I follow him into the small office space. It's tastefully decorated, with an understated nautical theme. Calming blues and crisp whites. A framed image of a rolling wave.

"I thought you don't spend a lot of time here," I blurt out, wondering why I haven't met him before last night when he obviously works from this office.

"I'm usually around a lot more," he clarifies. "The past few months have been an exception. Take a seat." He points to the chair in front of his desk.

I sit down and wait as he settles his large body into the chair across from mine. He's an imposing man but he has a compassionate glint in his eyes that puts me at ease.

Dex sighs. "I spoke to Devy. I know you're a fantastic server and have great rapport with a lot of the customers. Natural likeability."

"Thank you."

"But you can't work here if you're going out, getting blitzed, and driving drunk." His voice is steel.

"I know," I say quietly.

"Not because I'm a hard ass, but because you're better than that. And there are better ways to cope with your stuff."

My eyebrows pull together as I stare at him.

Dex sighs again. He steeples his hands in front of his face.

I wait for his sentencing. He said he wouldn't fire me but that was last night. Now that he's had more time to think it over, is going to cut me loose?

"You remind me of me," he says, surprising me.

"What?" I rear back.

He grins. "A little lost, a little lonely, a little rattled," he lists, unnerving me.

I meet his gaze and clamp my mouth shut, not confirming, or denying his assessment.

"That door," he points to his office door, "is always open. To everyone who works for me. To every customer that comes into Beirut. I've been around the block a few times. I've had my fair share of struggles. I know what it's like to be lost and lonely and rattled. And I hate seeing when other people are going through it. But I promise you, there are better ways to handle it. You need to talk? You need to blow off steam? You need to vent or get another opinion or toss ideas against a sounding board? Use that door. Not the bottle, not the pills, and not my parking lot to puke your guts up in. Cool?"

I stare at him. Is he letting me off this easy? Is he really giving me another shot? "Cool," I agree.

Dex grins. "Great. Want to grab a coffee and a bite?"

I frown, wondering if that's necessary. But my stomach chooses that moment to grumble.

Dex chuckles. I sigh.

"Sure," I agree.

He unfolds his frame from behind his desk. I move toward the door, and he follows. We exit from the back door into the bright afternoon sunshine and fall into step as we move toward a little diner on the corner.

"Tell me about yourself, Allegra," Dex makes conversation easily. In some ways, he reminds me of Buck.

I open my mouth, and without meaning to, start to confide in him. "I was born in Massachusetts, outside of Boston..."

TWO
DEREK

THE WHEELS of the plane touch down in LA and I roll my shoulders back and crack my neck.

"You slept the whole flight," Mav comments beside me.

"Yup," I mutter, not in the mood for a conversation. To discourage him from starting one, I power on my phone and stare at the screen.

Mav sighs beside me.

The screen lights up and a barrage of emails and texts comes through.

One catches my eye and I tap it.

It's a text from my manager, Jess.

Jess: The man, Derek Madden, that's claiming to be your father reached out again via his lawyer. He must have seen that you're in LA this weekend for the River Wells launch. He wants to meet.

I scoff. What a shit show. I've been in LA for forty-three seconds and already, I regret coming.

I'm part owner of a whiskey label that's doing a West Coast launch. Clearly, I have to show up for the festivities and the event. The timing is shitty, with fucking Levi checking into rehab less than seventy-two hours ago.

I drag a hand over my face.

And now, my so-called father, who bounced before I was born, wants to meet.

Me: Tell him to fuck off and stop contacting me.

I send the message and slip my phone back into my pocket, too annoyed to read any of the other unimportant messages.

"To grab brunch?" Mav looks at me expectantly.

"Huh?" I look up, realizing I caught the tail end of his question. "What brunch?"

He narrows his eyes. "I asked if you wanted to have brunch with me and Allegra on Sunday."

Allegra.

Just her name rips through me like a bullet, causing an invisible wound to spread across my chest. The rate of my breathing increases and I feel things, messy, complicated *feelings*, pouring from the gaping hole in my heart. "No," I snap, even though it couldn't be further from the truth.

I'm desperate to see Allegra. To get eyes on her and know she's okay. Better than okay; thriving, living, blossoming. I want to know she's doing all the things she would have missed out on if she came on tour.

I want the affirmation that I didn't ruin her because letting her go saved her.

But fuck, I can't see her. It would gut me.

The anger in her eyes, the disgust in the curve of her lip, the hatred—it would fucking gut me.

"Your loss," Mav mutters. "I'm also getting drinks with some friends tonight if you want to roll through."

"Whatever."

Another heavy sigh. "You know, I didn't have to come this weekend."

"You're right," I agree. He didn't have to come.

He could have begged off like Jameson or checked himself into fucking rehab like Levi.

"Fuck, you're stubborn," Mav replies, not at all offended.

Another truth.

I'm being shitty. It was thoughtful of Mav to tag along and support me in a new venture. I should be thankful he's here. Grateful to have a friend like him.

Instead, I'm sour as hell because I'm in the same goddamn city as Allegra and I can't see her.

I won't.

I'm here for work. I don't have time for distractions. I allowed Allegra to distract me, to get in my head, all damn summer and look how that turned out.

Her brother's in rehab, our tour was cut short, and she probably hates me on a cellular level.

The plane taxis and Maverick and I stand, stretch, and disembark.

When I clear the plane, retrieve my luggage, and step out into the sunny afternoon, I take stock of my mental well-being.

I'm exhausted and burnt out. My eyes feel scratchy and my head thrums. As incredible as our European fans are and as disappointed as I am in Levi, I can't squash the flicker of relief that our tour is officially done.

I need the time out. The quiet. The calm.

LA isn't any of those fucking things but it's a step up from screaming fans in London and sold-out shows in Berlin.

"You ready?" Mav calls out, holding open a door to a black Suburban.

"Yeah," I mutter, stowing my suitcase in the trunk and sliding into the back seat beside him.

Our driver points the SUV in the direction of my LA condo. I turn my head to stare out the window, to watch as the cityscape, the day, blurs past.

I'm in Allegra's city and still, I feel so far from her we may as well be on different planets.

"REIGN!" a woman squeals when she sees me. Her friends immediately flock and I dutifully turn and smirk.

"Ladies..." I dip my head to greet them. "Thanks for coming."

"As if we'd miss your launch!" the one wearing the skimpiest fucking top I've ever seen exclaims. She clutches her breasts dramatically and I briefly wonder if there's going to be a nip slip. "We're so happy you're here!"

Nope, no luck.

"Me too," I mutter.

"A photo," the event photographer reminds me.

I slip my hands into my pockets so I won't have to touch any of these women. They don't get the hint and drape themselves over my frame, rubbing up against me as much as humanly possible.

Snap.

"Thanks," I repeat. "Make sure you try the whiskey."

"Oh." The woman in the red miniskirt wrinkles her nose. "We don't drink whiskey."

"Of course not," I sigh, walking away. "It's just an event for a fucking whiskey label."

"There you are, mate," my River Wells partner, Johan Hansen, smacks me on the back. He's a tall, imposing, Viking type of guy. Blond hair, bushy eyebrows, steel blue eyes. He hails from Norway but maintains ties to Boston since his cousin, Torsten, is a former NHL player for the Hawks. Can't get away from this fucking hockey team no matter how hard I try.

But Johan's a decent guy and a solid partner. "What's good?"

"Glad you made it in time."

"Yeah," I agree, walking over to a high-top table.

He snags us each tumblers of whiskey and passes me one.

We clink glasses. "To River Wells," I say simply.

"River Wells," he echoes.

We drink to the success of our new label. I nearly polish off my drink in a few hearty gulps.

"Slow down," Johan warns. "Or you won't make it to the after party."

"Right," I say. Of course, there's an after party. It's so fucking LA, I want to laugh.

I glance at Johan, wondering if he really likes it here. He comes from serious money, the kind I couldn't fathom as a kid. I glance around the beautiful venue, filled with insipid, uninteresting women and guys looking to get their dicks wet.

At some point, this shit must grow old, right?

Hell, I'm in my goddamn prime, just stepped off a flight from Madrid, and I'm fucking bored by it all.

Unimpressed. Uninspired.

What the hell's the point anymore?

"You all right?" Johan peers at me closely.

"Yeah, sorry, man. Just jet lag."

"Of course. I'm sorry to hear about Levi." He lowers his voice respectfully. See what I mean? He's decent.

"It was a long time coming," I comment, speaking the truth. Not that people outside of our circles know the extent of Levi's addiction issues, but alcohol is only the tip of the iceberg.

"Yeah," Johan replies, taking a swig of whiskey. "You know, with the band complications and things being unsettled, you could stay here and help me grow the label. Be more involved with the day-to-day."

I cut him a look. Johan has been trying from the jump to get me to move out, or at least, spend more time in LA. But, "It's not for me, man. I gotta get back to Boston. To making music. This shit, Levi, the shortened tour—it will blow over."

Johan dips his head in understanding. "Just a thought. Another option."

I nod in thanks and take a sip of my whiskey. Damn, it's good. A flicker of pride swells in my chest that I helped create this label, that I weighed in on the whiskey I'm currently drinking.

"Hey! Congrats on the turnout." Mav steps to our table and grins.

Johan holds out a hand, which Mav shakes before pulling Johan into a hug.

Johan snorts. "Thanks for coming, Maverick."

"Wouldn't miss it," Mav says, shooting me a look.

I smirk, knowing he's taking a dig at me.

He grins back, knowing I know.

Fucking Mav. It's impossible to stay annoyed with him. He's too damn genuine.

"I've got some friends rolling through in a bit," Mav states, glancing at Johan. "All good?"

"What's your expression? The more the merrier?" Johan asks.

Mav laughs. "You got it. Yeah, cool. We're going to grab drinks, but what better place to start?"

"Exactly," Johan chuckles. "Begin your night with whiskey and see where it goes."

"Sideways," I mutter, but both Mav and Johan, used to my moodiness, ignore me, and continue their conversation.

I get another drink, mill about the space, mingle when I'm required to engage. The sky darkens as night falls. The smokiness of cigars hangs in the air, even though we're outside, on a rooftop. Still, oversized leather armchairs are clustered in groups and high-top tables decorate the perimeter.

It's as if someone took the library of a hyper-masculine, egotistical alpha and put it outside. But it lends a vivid experience to the whiskey and as I swirl my tumbler, I take a seat in a wingback chair and scan the event.

There's a good turnout, we're getting great press, and I'm excited to venture into a new business. Still, I can't shake the unease that rides low in my gut. I can't fully enjoy this moment, or this event, because my mind is twisted up on something else.

Allegra.

I start when my eyes fasten on her. She steps onto the rooftop as if bidden by my thoughts.

My gaze darts from her to Mav and I catch him staring straight at me.

He shrugs, completely unapologetic.

Fuck. I tip my head back and close my eyes.

She's here. Of course, Mav fucking invited her. But why the hell did she come?

My eyes spring open and I zero in on her.

She's as gorgeous as I remember but different.

I sit up straighter in my chair, my tumbler forgotten on a side table. My hands grip the armrests, my fingernails making indents in the buttery leather.

Everything is different.

Her long, dark hair has been chopped into a blunt bob and dyed. She's fucking blonde! If I didn't memorize the curves of her body, or intimately know the allure of her eyes, I wouldn't have recognized her.

Her lips are painted a dark red when the woman I recall from summer was usually fresh-faced and makeup free.

This version isn't wearing flip-flops or Chucks. She's rocking heels and a skintight bodycon dress that leaves nothing to the imagination. Every curve is on display. She turns toward Mav and I groan at her full, round ass.

She's here to torture me. That has to be it.

I growl as Mav's hand slides over her lower back. He hugs her tightly before kissing her cheek. They exchange words, and I try to read Mav's lips like a fucking loser.

What the hell is he saying?

He flips his chin in my direction and Allegra turns.

When she sees me, she freezes. Her lips part and her eyes widen. A shock of hurt, a ripple of regret, a mask of indifference. Emotions filter over her face and because I'm staring right at her, drinking her in, I catch each one in real time.

She turns back to Mav, dismissing me.

I chuckle, more surprised than anything else.

Yeah, she hates my guts.

And hell yeah, my blood still sings for her.

But fuck if she doesn't keep me on my toes. Catch me off guard. Call me out on my bullshit.

I'm still in fucking love with Allegra Rousell. Not that she ever knew it.

But now, the woman who used to look at me with hearts and hope in her gaze is more likely to chuck daggers at my head.

Yeah, I should've stayed on the damn plane.

THREE
ALLEGRA

"YOU DIDN'T TELL me he'd be here," I say, annoyed with Maverick but not surprised.

His blue eyes widen in surprise, whether from my appearance or my accusatory directness, I'm not sure.

My friend sighs and grips the back of his neck. "Because I knew you wouldn't come."

I raise my eyebrows sardonically. "You'd be right. And that would be my choice to make."

Mav sighs and his eyes narrow. "You're right; I'm sorry. But I'm glad you came, A. I miss you."

At the sincerity in his tone, my anger cools. It's not Mav's fault the band left without me. After I woke up, alone, in the brownstone and realized they left for tour, I was devastated.

Then, furious.

But when I stopped by the group home to check up on the kids and make sure they were processing Buck's death, Dre told me what he knew.

Derek said you're sticking around for the funeral before meeting the guys in Europe.

Derek's a motherfucking liar.

The thought whipped through my mind, but I didn't voice it. Not then, and not now.

Call it pride. Call it pain. Call it whatever the hell you want but I don't do more than purse my lips at Mav. "Miss you too."

"Thanks for being here." He slugs an arm around my shoulder and turns me toward a high-top table. Pressing a tumbler of whiskey into my hand, Mav kisses my temple. "I like your hair; you look good as a blonde."

I snort and raise the amber liquid to my lips, taking a swig. "I heard they have more fun."

"Is it true?" Humor lines his words.

"You tell me." I glance up at my friend and feel a little steadier with him by my side. Deep down, I know Mav wouldn't have ditched me if Derek hadn't painted a believable story for my absence. Mav reached out before Levi and continued to do so over the past four months.

He even messaged to check in after the news broke that my brother is in rehab.

"I always have fun, A."

"True," I cede the point.

"How are you finding life as a blonde?" he asks curiously.

"So far, it's all I hoped it would be." I give him the truth, bumping my hip against his. Being blonde has become my armor. A new look, paired with a new style, has given me the confidence I require to meet each day head-on. Mav chuckles but I catch the flash of concern in his gaze. I roll my eyes in response. "I'm good, Mav. Really."

"Okay," he agrees, lifting his glass. "Bottoms up, A."

"Cheers." I clink my glass with his and down the contents, even though it's not a shot.

Now that Derek is here, I need the courage and excuses alcohol provides. It will strengthen my resolve, let me hold on to my anger, and give me the perfect excuse to dip out early.

I smile and accept another tumbler from a passing server.

"Take it easy, A," Mav warns, glancing over his shoulder. I'm sure he's looking for Derek, but I don't care what either of them thinks.

I take another swig of whiskey.

"Allegra Rousell." A guy I recognize approaches, squinting at me. "That you?"

"Ethan," I laugh, greeting a fellow UCLA student. I haven't seen him since junior year when we had a sociology course together. Back then, I had long, brown hair and wore cardigans. Of course, he doesn't recognize me. Right now, I'm delighted to see him. "Hey!"

"Hey, girl." He wraps an arm around my waist and kisses my cheek.

"I didn't know you were coming tonight," I gush, gripping his shoulders with both hands.

He pulls back slightly and gives me a confused look. Of course, I wouldn't know he was coming; we haven't talked since before summer. Since before I blew up my life. Still, I widen my eyes at him and hope he'll play along.

"It was a last-minute thing," he tosses out, correctly reading the desperation in my gaze.

Thank you, Ethan!

I snuggle closer into his side, and he palms the center of my back.

Mav watches me closely, his eyebrows pulled together, his mouth a thin line.

"Mav, this is Ethan. Ethan, Mav." I do the introductions without informing either man what the other means to me.

Close friend who hurt me meet random classmate coming to my rescue.

"Hey, man." Mav holds out a hand.

"Maverick Tate," Ethan says. "Damn, it's good to meet you. I didn't realize you rolled like this, Allegra."

I chuckle. "Yeah, well, you know me, Ethan."

"Mm-hmm," my friend agrees, giving me a smirk.

He thinks I'm playing hard to get for Mav's sake. It's preferable to the truth. That I am desperate to hurt Derek, to make him jealous, to make him react, anything so he can taste a sliver of the pain he caused me.

Let him think I moved on. Let him think I'm happy and secure with a new man. Ethan, with his ripped jeans and fitted, plain gray shirt, and half-sleeves of swirling ink looks the part. He's several inches taller than me and has a broad, athletic build. With curly brown hair and laughing green eyes, he plays the part well.

"You know each other well?" Mav asks, gesturing between us with his tumbler.

"Well enough," I reply, snaking my arm around Ethan's waist. I look up at him. "Right, babe?"

Ethan rolls his lips together to keep from laughing. "Of course." He gives Mav a sheepish look. "Things are still pretty new, but every moment I spend with Allegra is a beautiful surprise."

I snort lightly as Ethan's eyes dance with mirth.

Tapping his hip, I tip my head toward the bar. "Better get you a drink."

"Nice meeting you, man," Ethan says to Mav.

Mav's eyes dart between Ethan and me. "Same. Say something before you bounce, A."

"Of course," I agree breezily, leading my fake man to the bar.

"What the hell, Allegra?" Ethan mutters when we're out of earshot. "Are you seriously trying to make Maverick Tate jealous?"

I order him a whiskey.

"Not at all," I whisper back. "Things are just...complicated at the moment." I turn pleading eyes at him. "Will you give me a ride home tonight?"

"Of course," he sighs. "Are you okay? I haven't seen you since last year. Last I heard, you took a leave of absence."

"Well, I'm back now." I polish off my whiskey and signal to the bartender that I'll take another.

"And blonde."

"That too." I grin at Ethan.

He snorts and shakes his head. "Whatever. I've got to catch up with some friends, but signal if you need me. I'll be around and I won't take off without you."

"Thank you, Ethan."

He nods.

The bartender places down our tumblers and we clink them together before drinking.

"You gonna be okay?" Ethan asks. His concern wraps around me like a hug, and I nod, grateful for his presence. For the friendship he's showing me.

"Yes. Go mingle." I give him a playful shove.

"Okay. Signal." He flutters his fingers underneath his chin like we have a secret code, and I laugh.

"I will," I promise, returning the signal.

Ethan winks.

I watch him move through the crowd, meet up with a group of guys I don't know.

Sighing, I turn back toward my tumbler and gasp. I clutch my heart and glare at Derek.

"What do you want?" I bite out.

"You're still easy to sneak up on," he remarks, his face a cool mask of indifference.

His demeanor may be cool, but his whiskey eyes are molten, blazing hot and angry, with a possessive edge that sends a thrill up my spine.

I shrug and feign disinterest as I take a sip of my drink. I smack my lips together and check him out, not bothering to hide my perusal.

Damn Derek for looking so delectable. Europe was too good to him.

He put on muscle in the months since I last saw him. His biceps are bigger, his shoulders broader. His hair is longer, and I long to run my fingers through it. I yearn to reach for him but force my fingers to curl into my palm instead.

His jaw is tight, and I know he's angry, his energy radiating the type of danger that pulls me closer.

My body awakens under his hard gaze and heat rolls through my veins.

Even though I'm mentally rioting, my body craves Derek's touch. His approval. It's sick and I turn away, closing my eyes as I take a hearty swig of whiskey.

"I'm sorry about Levi," he offers, his voice raspy.

I shrug.

"Why'd you come, Allegra?" he asks, dipping his head to catch my eyes.

Part of me hates that he doesn't call me Stellina; part of me hates that he addresses me at all.

"This is my city, Reign," I remind him, using his famous moniker to create distance between us. To remind myself that I will not fall for his heartbreaking eyes and soulful rasp again. "Why are you here?"

He flips his chin. "This is my event."

Oh. I glance around the space, tastefully decorated and thoughtfully curated. He owns a whiskey label? "Congratulations," I mutter, lifting my tumbler in his direction before taking another drink. I wish I hated the taste of River Wells, but like all things Derek, it's delicious.

Derek's hand darts out and he pulls the glass from my fingers, placing it on the bar forcefully. Whiskey splashes over the rim and dots the bar in teardrops.

"Who's the guy?" Derek demands.

I chew the corner of my mouth to stop my grin. He saw my exchange with Ethan, and he doesn't like it.

Too fucking bad.

I tilt my head and give him a mocking look. "Why? There are no house rules here," I say, mentioning his dumb no-boy rule when I lived at the brownstone.

As if I was going to hook up with a random when I was so hung up on him.

"Who is he, Allegra?"

I laugh. "None of your business, Derek."

He narrows his eyes. Lifting his hand, he tugs on a strand of my hair. "You've changed."

I smile, a real one this time. He's right. I've wised up and hardened my heart. "That's funny, because you're exactly the same."

FOUR

DEREK

I WANT to break the motherfucker's hand as it slips across Allegra's waist.

"You ready to head out?" he asks her quietly. He disregards me completely and my anger ricochets through my limbs like the ball in a pinball game.

Allegra looks up at him, her blonde tresses brushing across his chin. Their interaction is intimate, their familiarity comfortable.

I grip my tumbler tighter, wishing the glass would shatter in my palm. Wanting something to ruin this moment where my girl—the one that I can't get over—grins up at another like he hung the fucking moon and strung the stars.

Stellina. She's my star.

"Sure," she replies, wriggling her fingers at him from beneath her chin and giving him an almost-secret smile.

He taps her hip once with his hand. "I'll go say bye to my boys."

"Meet you at the entrance," she agrees.

The dude lopes off. I glare at his retreating back and it pains me that I see it. Her attraction to him. He looks like a good guy. He's not clean-cut or wearing a letterman jacket or anything, but he doesn't radiate emotionally unavailable either.

Allegra turns her attention back to me. A streak of sadness blurs her expression for an instant before she blocks it. Blinks it away and resumes her glare of scorn. "Good luck with everything, Reign."

"Stop calling me that," I snap. Why won't she say Derek?

She smirks, the corners of her mouth pinching. "What do you want me to call you? I'm just another girl who fell for your tortured eyes and raspy voice only to be left the morning after." She shrugs. "I'm no one to you."

"Allegra, fuck. Come on, that's not true," I growl, leaning closer as if to cower her into acceptance. Into submission.

She chuckles, the sound hard. "Yeah, it is. At least now, I know it." She lifts her chin at me, her eyes flashing. "Enjoy the rest of your night."

She moves to slip around me, but I grasp her bicep, squeeze enough to make her halt.

She turns her head slowly, her eyes glinting with amusement, her eyebrow arching in a challenge.

What the fuck? Where is the woman who would've lashed out at me by now? The one who would've given me a clue on her feelings? Hell, she used to weave them through her expressions.

This version of Allegra gives away nothing but thinly veiled bitterness and an attitude I can't get enough of.

"What are you going to do? Now?" I ask. Is she happy back in LA? Is she taking classes? Does she need any support with what's happening with Levi?

The questions hover on the tip of my tongue, but I don't

know how to voice them. I don't know how to be the guy she needs in this moment because I don't know what the hell she needs.

There aren't tears or helplessness. There's no hurt in her expression or longing in her eyes.

My girl is locked up tighter than Simon's prison cell.

She cocks her head. "I'm gonna go home and let Ethan fuck me," she replies, her tone devoid of malice. In fact, it's empty of nearly all emotion. She's stating a fact. "Hard."

Allegra pulls her arm from my grasp and moves toward the entrance.

I slap the top of the bar. The sting traveling up my arm does nothing to quench my fury. I need to destroy something tangible, like fucking Ethan, in order to cool this horror.

My chest burns. The feelings, emotions, that stick to my ribs like plaque clench, tight enough to make my stomach roil. I drag my fingers through my hair, tugging to erase the vivid images that now flicker through my mind.

Ethan kissing Allegra. His hands caressing her body. His fingers dipping into her secret places.

Places meant for me. My hands, my eyes, my mouth.

"Fuck," I swear, swinging back to the bartender.

Smart man already filled another tumbler and added a shot of tequila. I down it instantly.

"How's it going, man?" Mav approaches hesitantly.

I whip my head to glare at him. "What the fuck were you thinking? Why the hell did you invite her here?"

"I'm worried about her," Mav states. His elbow bumps mine and he jerks his head to indicate we should both face forward, stare at the bar.

Bartender deserves a fucking raise because he steps to the other side and begins to clean spotless glasses.

"What are you talking about?" I snap.

"She's off, man. Something...something's off."

"She's completely different," I agree. I fucking broke her. Destroyed her innocence, stomped on her vulnerability, abandoned her.

The truth settles in my stomach, layering like sediments until it reaches the base of my throat and I want to vomit it up. Expel it all so I don't have to live with it. With the regrets and the goddamn *knowing*.

I devastated Allegra. I started to snuff my Stellina out.

"I'm worried about her," Mav repeats.

I glance at my bandmate, and note the tightness of his expression, the shadows that pass through his gaze. When I don't respond, he continues. "I kept in touch with her."

"What?" I ask. They've been talking this whole time? And Mav never let on how she was doing? Never said she was okay, back in LA.

"She's my friend, Derek." He glares at me. "And I knew she had a tough time with Buck's passing, but I also know what I saw that night. She—fuck, man—she cared for you. A lot. And you stepped aside for the sake of the band, and I know that was hard."

Fuck him for speaking of me and Allegra in the past.

"It was hard for you," he continues. "And it had to be hard for her. She's not okay, man."

I tap the bar with two fingers. The bartender's eyes jump to mine.

"Tequila," I say.

He nods and pours two shots.

"You think she's spiraling?" I wonder, considering her appearance, her interaction with Ethan. She was nothing like the woman who knocked on the door of our brownstone at the start of summer.

"I think she's struggling," Mav amends. "Thanks, mate." He tells the bartender before downing the shot. Smacking his lips together, he turns to me. "I'm gonna stay in LA for a bit. Jameson's back in Boston with Amelia, band stuff is up in the air while Levi recovers..."

"No Costa Rica?" I taunt, knowing it's Mav's favorite place to disappear.

"Not yet," he replies. "I won't let Allegra down the way I did Levi."

Shit. "That's not your fault, man," I tell him the truth, but I feel his guilt. The same remorse swims in my veins.

We were too busy getting caught up in the fame vortex, getting lost in the music, getting fucked up in the vibe, that we turned a blind eye to Levi's struggles. And now, our rhythm guitarist is detoxing in rehab. Not just for alcohol, the way the media believes, but for drugs. For sex. For straight-up addiction.

"I'm sticking around," Mav repeats, resolve heavy in his tone.

"You do you." I take my shot.

Mav smacks the bar top lightly. "I'm out. Gonna meet up with some friends. See you back at the condo?"

"Sure," I agree.

I hang at the bar for another beat. Polish off my tumbler. Then, I turn and locate Johan.

With Mav's words echoing in my mind and Allegra's scorn souring my stomach, I flip my chin at my business partner.

"Having fun, Reign?" Johan grins.

"I wanted to run something by you," I say.

"Sure."

"Been doing some thinking." I tilt my head toward the

bar I've been posted up beside for the better part of the past hour.

"Ah, the blonde vixen caught your eye?"

I narrow my gaze at Johan and his grin widens.

"We have history," I admit, not divulging details.

His grin slips and understanding colors his expression. "Ah."

"I'd like to stay in LA longer than I planned."

"It will be great to have your help in expanding our label," he replies, giving me the out I'm searching for. Offering me a real reason, an excuse, in a heartbeat.

"That would be great. Thanks, Johan."

Johan smacks a hand on my shoulder. "Of course. We're partners, Derek."

"Right," I agree.

Johan turns back toward the conversation he excused himself from. I spend the remainder of the evening promoting the brand, discussing the label, and posing for selfies.

But Johan's words stick with me.

Partners.

Save for the band, I've been on my own for a long time. I don't have family or partnerships or many friends.

I have my bandmates and Dre. Full stop.

Then, my lawyer Aiden, my manager Jess, and my publicist Kimberly.

And now, maybe Johan.

The realization eases some of the pressure in my chest. I can stay in LA. I can show up for Allegra.

Because the blonde vixen has caught more than my eye.

She's demanded my full attention, and this time, I'm not going anywhere.

I'll prove I'm the man who should be in her bed, and in her heart.

Not fucking Ethan.

FIVE

ALLEGRA

"SO, it's not one, but two, of The Burnt Clovers?" Ethan lifts a wry eyebrow as he idles by the curb in front of my place.

I sigh and roll my head along the headrest. "It's complicated."

"Your life seems that way, Allegra."

I snort and turn to glance at my classmate-turned-friend. "Thanks for helping me out back there."

"Of course," he replies. Then, more seriously, "What's going on with you?"

I shrug. "The usual. It was a whirlwind summer and I'm getting my feet back underneath me."

"Not living with Nova and the girls?"

"I wasn't planning to be back on campus this semester," I sigh. "But now that I am—" I pause and gesture to the small apartment building where I'm renting a studio. "I'm serving at Beirut and doing some work with a homelessness NGO downtown."

Ethan looks impressed and some of my nerves dissipate.

The last thing I need is another well-meaning friend looking out for me. Worrying.

Nova, Kenny, and Ivy have done enough clucking over me, asking questions, and extending olive branches. I don't need to add Ethan to the list.

"Cool," he replies, shifting his grip on the steering wheel. "That's good, Allegra."

"Yeah," I agree. "I went to Boston to figure out some things career wise," I admit, shutting down the flicker of pain that works through my chest at the thought of Buck. "And I did. Now, I'm back, putting some of that into motion and taking classes when I can."

Ethan nods. "Honestly, I'm glad to hear it. And I'm glad to see you tonight. You look good."

I grin. "Thanks, Ethan." I reach for the door handle. "Thanks for the ride and for looking out. I appreciate you."

He snorts and shakes his head. "Anytime. Hey, don't be such a stranger." He passes me his phone. "Let me get your number. We should chill sometime now that I don't see you on campus."

"Sure." I punch my digits into his phone and save the contact under Hottest Girl I Know.

Passing it back to Ethan, I lean over to brush a kiss over his cheek. "Good night, Ethan."

"See you around, Allegra."

I walk to the front of my building, the cool breeze skating over my bare legs and shoulders. Once I make it inside, Ethan pulls away from the curb and I enter my tiny apartment.

I exhale and let the stress from the evening drain from my limbs. I pour myself a glass of wine and kick back on the couch, my eyes closing. Mentally, I flip through moments from the day.

My meeting with Dex. Talking.

A hot yoga class.

And then, from the night.

Mav. Derek. Ethan.

Concern. Anger. Worry.

What a fucking shit show.

My phone beeps and I glance at the screen.

Unknown: I better be the Hottest Guy I Ever Met in your phone.

I laugh and take a sip of my wine.

Me: Thanks for the ride, Ethan.

Ethan: Sweet dreams.

Sweet dreams, Stellina. Derek's voice sounds in my ear.

Ugh. Before I toss my phone down, another message comes through on my girl group chat.

Nova: YOU SAW HIM? And you haven't messaged us yet...

Ivy: What gives, A?

*Me: I *just* got home.*

Kenny: How? Did you drive? Did you drink?

Me: Relax. I ran into Ethan from sociology.

Nova: Dresden? He's the best!

Ivy: Of course, you know him.

Nova: Not my fault you don't socialize.

Kenny: That was nice of him to give you a ride.

Nova: I'm surprised Reign didn't take you home...

Me: How do you even know I saw him?

Ivy: (image of me and Derek talking at the bar)

Me: Seriously? There are photos?

Nova: It's kind of cool that your life is legit news.

Me: It's not.

*Kenny: Social media gossip handles are *not* news.*

Ivy: They could be.

Kenny: What happened?

Me: He was pissed off that I was talking to Ethan.

Nova: YAY!

Ivy: Stop it!

Kenny: No apology? No explanation?

Me: No, nothing.

Kenny: Good riddance, Derek Reiner.

Nova: Nah, he's gonna win you back, A.

Me: (six laughing face emojis)

Me: He's in town for like a weekend...

Ivy: Bet you he extends his trip now.

Nova: Totally.

Kenny: Doesn't he have work?

Nova: Please. He can afford to take off and woo our girl.

Me: I don't want to be "wooed."

Nova: I do.

Ivy: (emoji of girl raising her hand) Girl, same.

Kenny: (two eye roll emojis)

Nova: Let's do brunch tomorrow?

Me: I'd love to, but I made plans with Mav.

Kenny: I have an alumni lunch with some of my dad's old fraternity brothers tomorrow afternoon. Want to do a morning run?

Ivy: Fuck no!

Kenny: Come on, we could get coffee afterwards.

Nova: Doughnuts?

Kenny: I'll buy them.

Me: I haven't run in forever. I'd hold you all back.

Kenny: We'll do a beginner route.

Ivy: Fine. If A is in, I'll go.

Nova: Please, Allegra! We haven't seen you in years.

Me: It's been a week.

Nova: Exactly. It's been ages.

I snort to myself. I miss my friends. Coming back to LA after my summer in Boston was a tough transition. Everything is different now and I don't feel the same as when I left. I'm not the same person and my outlook is different. While my relationships with my friends have strained a bit, that's on me. They haven't stopped giving me their support and extending invitations to hang out.

I miss them. I miss the easy camaraderie we used to have. I miss living with them and hanging out late nights, talking about everything and anything.

Me: Okay.

Ivy: YES!

Nova: Our corner at 7a.m.?

Kenny: I'm in.

Me: See you girls there. XO

Kenny: Good night.

I drop my phone on the end table and take another pull from my wine glass. The bold red is delicious and soothes the tension I've carried around all day. Knowing I need a good night's rest, especially if I'm going to meet the girls early to run, have brunch with Mav, head downtown to the NGO headquarters, and work a shift at Beirut tomorrow night, I get off my ass to swipe the sleeping pills I jacked from a girl I work with.

I shake two out of the container and hold them in the palm of my hand.

It's normal to need a little assistance to get good z's when one is burning both ends of the candle the way I am. Self-medicating is better than no-medicating, right?

Shaking my head at myself, I pop the tablets into my mouth and wash them down with a swig of wine. Then, I plop down in front of the TV and turn on a new matchmaking show on Netflix. As I get caught up in the various storylines and dramas playing out on screen, it dulls the real dramas of my life. The pills and wine slow my thoughts. My shoulders fall, my neck drops back, and my eyes close.

Slowly, I drift off to sleep. My body is peacefully numb. My mind, finally quiet.

There are no thoughts of Derek. No anger toward Mav. No resentment for Levi.

No excuses for my friends or worries over my classes. No grief for Buck.

There's nothing but an empty expanse that stretches long and far, infinitely. I slip into it and let it pull me under.

Relief fills my veins.

I WAKE the next morning with a start.

"Shit," I mutter, gripping the back of my neck.

Falling asleep on the couch wasn't my best idea since I've got a crick in my neck and a wine stain on my couch.

"Fuck." I glare at the red patch for good measure.

Checking my phone, I groan when I realize the time. It's already 9 a.m. and I've missed the run. Glancing down at my bodycon dress from last night, I know I need a shower.

I reach for my phone and wince when I read the texts from my friends.

Kenny: I'm on our corner.

Nova: Allegra!! Are you coming?

Ivy: Girl, where you at?

Kenny: Are you okay?

Nova: Don't bail on us again, A. I cancelled an 8 a.m. tutoring session and my TA is so many chili peppers hot.

Ivy: Are you still coming? Do you want us to wait?

Kenny: We went for a run! Sorry, I need to get ready for that alumni lunch. Talk to you later.

Nova: We already got doughnuts. Message us and let us know you're good.

Me: I'm so fucking sorry, guys. I overslept.

Ivy: Again?

Nova: Not cool, A. This is like the third time you've bailed on us.

Me: I'm really sorry. I swear it won't happen again.

Crickets because, no one believes me.

Shit, I don't believe myself.

Heaving out a sigh, I drag myself up and throw myself into a shower. The hot water washes away some of my grogginess. I'll make it up to the girls. But right now, I've got to get ready to meet Mav. Then, my volunteer work with the NGO. And end the night at Beirut.

I don't have time to worry about my friends' feelings. It was a mistake, an accident, and I'll do better next time.

I blow dry my hair and dress quickly. I grab an energy drink on my way out the door and head to the restaurant for brunch.

Ethan: (sends link: Are things heating up between our favorite rockstar and his bandmate's little sister?)

I groan. It's another photo of me and Derek at the bar last night. From this angle, Derek looks pissed, and I look… well, starstruck. The way I always feel around him.

Ethan: It's ridiculous what people publish.

I exhale, relieved he's not buying into the story even though I feel its truth rattle around my veins.

Me: So dumb.

Ethan: It was great to see you last night. Want to grab a coffee if you're on campus tomorrow?

Me: I'd love to, but I have work after class. Rain check?

Ethan: I'm holding you to that.

I grin as a flutter shimmies down my rib cage. Biting my bottom lip, I think about what it would feel like to kiss Ethan Dresden. Would he push the memory of Derek from my mind? Would he erase Derek's taste from my lips?

Can he help me move on the way I've been trying to since I woke up in Derek's bed, alone and heartbroken?

I slide my phone into my back pocket and head toward the restaurant.

God, I hope so.

SIX

DEREK

I CROSS the quad as soon as she exits the building. I'm out of my element here, surrounded by the educated and elite. I barely graduated high school and wonder sometimes if my teachers didn't pass me my senior year to push me through the system.

Music saved my life, every step of the way.

Glancing at my watch, I note the professor dismissed Allegra's class early. Good thing I was here, waiting and watching, or I would have missed her. Good thing Mav filled me in on the pieces of her life he learned when they had brunch yesterday, or I wouldn't have known to show up this morning.

She rolls her eyes when she spots me. "What are you doing here?"

"How was your class? Social Justice and Equity sounds interesting." I hold out my peace offering, a cup of coffee. It's not much but I need to ease into this new normal with Allegra.

It's clear she doesn't want to see me. It's obvious that I hurt her, deeply, and she wants nothing to do with me. But fuck if I'm going to turn my back on her when she's so damn...lost. Hardened. Nothing like my girl.

Except, she's *not* mine.

My molars grind together, and I force my attention back to her pretty face. Even now, when she's scowling at me, she's so gorgeous, it's hard to look right at her. Like staring at the sun, she's likely to burn my damn retinas.

"Stalker much?" she replies, swiping the coffee cup and taking a swig.

"Look." I stuff my hands in my pockets and rock back on my heels. I am so far out of my comfort zone, my stomach clenches, and the back of my neck prickles. I don't know how to do this shit. I'm not Maverick Tate. Hell, even Levi is better at navigating emotions, having grown up with Allegra as his sister.

Allegra raises a sardonic eyebrow, unimpressed and waiting.

"I'm sorry," I mutter. The words leave a sour film in my mouth.

"For which part, Derek?" Allegra pops her hip, tilting her head at me.

I sigh, glancing around the quad. Students mill about, their backpacks slung over their shoulders, their fingers tapping out text messages, or hanging with their friends, laughing.

I can see Allegra here. Studying on a big blanket with her friends under the shade of an oak tree. Grabbing an iced coffee and reading in an oversized armchair in the library.

Hell, I can even see her dating a guy like the one she left with the other night. Ethan.

Is that what she wants now? Is that who this new version of my Stellina is attracted to?

I swear. "All of it, okay? I shouldn't have left the way I did."

"No, that was fucking cowardly," she spits. "But it's my bad for expecting more of you."

Ouch. As if her words contained a physical barb, I rub against the center of my chest.

Allegra's mask slips for an instant and in her eyes, I read a flicker of remorse. Relief fills my veins, allowing my shoulders to drop. She's still in there. The woman I care for still exists. The pain I caused buried her alive, and now, I need to dig her out.

Remind her who she is.

Make amends for the mess I caused.

"I hate seeing you like this," I admit.

"Like what? Having my own life and not hanging onto yours?" She tilts her head, but again, I note the pinch at the corners of her mouth. She's saucy as hell, but I wonder how much she likes the taste of her own spice.

"Hardened," I reply. "My Stellina is all light, too damn bright and burning too hot, but still, all light." I reach for her wrist, and she lets me take it. Pressing my thumb against her pulse, I love the way it flutters. For me. "Talk to me, Allegra. Tell me what you need. I'm right here and—"

"I don't need anything. Or anyone," she cuts me off, but her tone is softer than it was a second ago. Her vowels are rounded out now, less sure of herself. She shakes her head and pulls her arm back. "I gotta get to work."

"Where are you working?" I ask, even though I already know the answer. Thank you Mav and social media.

"An NGO that helps find housing for homeless people," she replies, squinting at me as if to gage my reaction.

I smile. It's so her, the desire to help, the constant

compassion. "Goes hand in hand with Social Justice and Equity, huh?" I remark.

She looks away and fidgets with the strap of her bag. "Don't stick around on my account, Derek. I wasn't kidding; I don't need you. Or Levi. I don't need anyone but myself."

With that, she strides away, moving toward the parking lot with measured, confident steps.

It's hard not to feel a flare of pride for her. As much as I hate her new devil-may-care attitude, she's always impressed me. I know she's tough; she's got grit. I just never had her anger—her pain—directed at me like this.

Pulling out my phone, I call Maverick.

"How's your stalking going?" He answers on the first ring.

I ignore that. "Get in touch with Allegra's friends, will you? I think they'll be more receptive to you than me."

He snorts. "Everyone is more receptive to me than you."

"Will you do it or not?"

"Yeah, man. I'm way ahead of you. It seems they're worried about Allegra too. She isn't living with them this semester and she's been blowing off their brunches and hangouts. Missed a run yesterday."

"Keep an eye on her, Mav. Something's not right," I say quietly, the truth eating at my stomach.

"No shit," he scoffs.

"I'm going to meet with Johan. I want to take on some of his day-to-day shit since I'm staying in town."

"You're staying for her, aren't you?" Curiosity burns behind his words, and I know he wants the truth. He wants to know I'm doing right by Allegra for all the times I did her dirty.

"Yeah," I clip out. My mouth is too dry. Fuck, why is

this so damn awkward? I clear my throat. "I'm staying for her."

"Good. I'll help you."

"I know."

"In another few weeks, Levi can see visitors," Mav changes the subject. "He's going to reach out once he's cleared."

Damn, these Rousell siblings are going to be the death of me.

"So soon?" I thought he needed to dry out longer before he could see anyone from the outside world.

"Yep. You up for a visit?"

I peer down the quad. Allegra is gone.

Levi is gone.

The hollowness that spread throughout my body during the tour widens, threatening to swallow me up.

"Yeah, man. I'm up for a visit."

"Cool. I'll make the arrangements once he's ready. See if I can get Jameson to fly out."

"Alright. I'll see you later, Mav."

"Later." He disconnects the call.

I slip my phone into my back pocket and move toward the parking lot. On my way, a familiar face pulls me up short.

Ethan.

He's leaning against a building, chatting with another guy. He dips his head down, biting his bottom lip, before glancing up and laughing at something the guy says. The guy reaches out and touches his hip before moving past him.

Huh? I narrow my eyes. Relief starts to lace through my limbs.

That was definitely flirting. Maybe Ethan is gay?

Maybe Allegra was playing me, pretending to be into him just to piss me off?

Ethan looks up and sees me staring at him. His expression changes, the playful smirk slipping as animosity moves over his face. He glares at me and lifts his chin, silently asking what the fuck I want.

I flip him off and walk away.

Nope, he's got a thing for my girl. He doesn't care if she's starting to spiral. He doesn't know her well enough to know that this woman—with the blonde bob and the skintight dress—isn't her.

I've known Allegra since she was seventeen years old. And yeah, I existed on the periphery for most of that time. But I know her heart. I've seen her soul.

I fucking fell in love with her.

I tried to save her from me, from the band. From life on tour, with the parties and the women and the drugs. The wildness of it and the man I become when I'm swept up in its current.

In doing so, I ruined her. I broke her. I gave her a tough exterior with a marshmallow center.

But now I'm back. I'm not going anywhere. Ethan won't win.

And I won't stop fighting for my Stellina.

SEVEN

ALLEGRA

DEX IS SITTING in his office, looking at the schedule, when I post up in the doorframe.

He looks up and smiles. "You're early."

"I got two people situated in their new homes today," I tell him proudly about my NGO work.

He holds out a fist and I step closer, bump my knuckles against his.

"What's the schedule look like?" I ask.

"I moved your shift. Wednesday instead of Tuesday."

I roll my eyes.

"You gotta study for that statistics exam," he reminds me.

At his concern, the stress I've been carrying around all week, the nerves that tightened and held, building pressure in my chest, release. Derek showed up on campus again, for the fourth time in two weeks, to hand me a coffee. To make small talk. To see me.

Today, he even had a little brown bag with a doughnut in it. I don't know what his angle is. I barely give him the time of day and still, he appears. What's worse is I find myself looking for him, hoping he'll surprise me.

I clearly have issues I need to work through.

I let out a long exhale and plop down in the chair in front of Dex's desk.

"What's going on?" he asks, leaning back in his chair.

It's strange how in only two weeks, Dex can read me better than Levi could for the past few years. Better than my parents. In that way, he reminds me of Buck.

I scrunch my nose, trying to quell the emotion that ripples behind my face at the thought of my old friend. Buck was a true friend.

"My ex is back in town," I admit, being candid with Dex. Again, he reminds me of Buck and the night Buck took me out for a burger and milkshake while I nursed some of my Derek-inflicted wounds.

That should have been a sign. A big, giant, red fucking flag.

Dex's eyebrows draw together. "He harassing you? Giving you a hard time?"

"No, no." I shake my head. "Nothing like that. He just... Hell, he's not even an ex. More like a summer fling gone wrong."

Dex snorts.

"He unnerves me," I admit. "He's popped by campus a few times to talk to me. Seeing him again..."

"Rattles you?"

"Yeah."

"Because you still have feelings for him?"

I shrug. Will I ever not have feelings for Derek? Highly unlikely. "I'm pissed at him."

Dex barks out a laugh. "I'd hate to be on the end of your ire, Allegra. But, this guy, he gonna be a problem?"

"No," I say. "Not the way you're thinking. I'm just...a little out of sorts today. I wasn't expecting him to show up on campus, and my friends are icing me out because of how many times I dropped plans with them," I sigh. Sometimes, talking to Dex is like going to confession. I tell him all the messed-up things I've done, and he gives me honest advice, devoid of judgement. After our chats, I feel better, even if I don't do the penance and make things right straightaway.

"Why'd you skip out on them?" He straightens in his chair and clicks the back of his pen. His gaze is more curious than anything else.

I shrug. "Last week, I overslept and missed a run. This week..." I shrug. "I forgot we made lunch plans."

Dex huffs, knowing I'm not giving him the whole story. I don't want to admit that I cut class and grabbed a liquid lunch of the alcoholic variety with some randoms I met at Beirut. "Want my advice?"

I wave a hand at him to continue.

"This thing with your ex, it will blow over one way or the other. Is he back in town because of you?"

"I think so," I admit. I know he has his new whiskey label, but Derek has his fingers in a lot of pies. More important than any business venture is his music, and he always heads home to Boston to work on it.

Why else would he stick around in LA, keep showing up on campus, and learn my class schedule, if not to annoy me?

I tilt my head, a new thought emerging. Maybe he stayed in town to apologize? Now that he's gotten it out of the way, gave me his peace offering of a coffee and dough-nut, will he bounce?

"Well," Dex continues, pulling me from my Derek-centered thoughts. What else is new? "If he's here for you, he'll either win you back or piss off when he learns there's no shot." Dex chuckles and points at me. "That depends on how you handle stuff with him. But it will blow over. On the other hand, your friends... You don't want to lose that, Allegra. Friends should always come first, especially if they're good friends who have your back."

"They are," I confirm.

"Then stop worrying about the guy and make things right with your girls." He glances down at the schedule. "You need your Friday night shift?"

I shake my head. "Not if tonight is solid."

Dex makes a change on the schedule. "Then you're off. Go out with your girls."

"Okay," I laugh. "I will." I stand from the chair. "Thanks, Dex."

"Anytime. And hey"—he catches my attention before I turn—"I'm proud of you. Two people settled today; that's great work, A."

I grin. "Thanks. I'm happy for them."

"You should be." He reaches into a drawer in his desk and tosses me a black, half-apron. "Tonight's gonna be slammed. Make your money because I don't want to see your face again until next week, after you ace that exam."

I nod, gripping the apron in my right hand. "All right. Thanks, Dex."

"See ya later, kid."

I leave his office and move toward the room that houses staff lockers. I stow my belongings and quickly change into my uniform. Tying the apron around my waist, I stop in front of the mirror to fix my hair and swipe on some lip gloss.

I like working at Beirut. It's a fun environment, it's good

money, and Dex has proven to be a solid mentor. In a way, he's stepping into the shoes my father never filled. He's giving my bullshit boundaries while not cutting my rope too much.

It should piss me off; instead, I look forward to it. I like that I can talk to him about anything. I like that he reminds me of Buck. Sometimes, I imagine Buck sent him to me, a kind, generous, father figure to keep me in check.

Pleased with my appearance, I move out to the floor. Within thirty minutes, my tables are packed, and the bar is three-deep with customers. I grin. Tonight will be a solid shift, taking the pressure off so I can enjoy Friday night out with my friends.

I HUSTLE MY ENTIRE SHIFT. When Beirut shuts down at 3 a.m., I breathe a sigh of relief and collapse against one of my tables.

"How'd you do, girl?" Devy calls out.

I mentally calculate the last round of checks I closed out. "I cleaned up."

Devy cheers. "Tonight was solid."

"Went by fast," Luis remarks.

I move toward the bar and slide onto a barstool. Devy fills me a glass of water. The crew assembles and we close out our registers, move to the lockers, gather our belongings, and say good night.

I don't see Dex again; he must have left already.

Luis walks me to my car, and I thank him for looking out.

"Drive safe, mama," he tells me, giving a mock salute.

I slip behind the steering wheel and turn the ignition. Leaning my head against the headrest, I close my eyes and suck in an inhale. Then, I find my phone in my bag and pull up the group chat.

Me: Sorry again about lunch. I know I flaked, and it was shitty of me. I'm not working Friday night. Drinks? First round is on me...

I don't expect anyone to respond right away since it's 3:30 a.m. so when my phone beeps, I'm surprised.

I glance at the screen.

Derek: You get home okay?

I sigh, shaking my head. Now, he's relentless? What about all summer when I was desperate for any morsel of attention he would drop my way?

I consider not responding but I know he knows I read his message. Not wanting him to think he affects me, I tap out a reply.

Me: On my way home now.

Derek: It's late.

No shit. I roll my eyes.

Derek: Why didn't you tell me you're cocktail serving?

Me: Didn't figure that out when you were pulling up my class schedule? Your game is weak sauce, Reign.

Derek: Message me when you get home.

Me: No. Stop bothering me.

Derek: Can't.

I snort and toss my phone into the cupholder. Then, I turn up the volume on a song I like and drive to my studio apartment.

As soon as I flip on the lights, a text comes through, making my phone buzz in my hand.

Derek: ...

Argh! He is so infuriating!

Me: I'm home! Happy now?

Derek: Sweet dreams, Stellina.

I glare at the screen, fuming. It's what he whispered in my ear before slipping from my life. What the hell is Derek playing at?

I plug in my phone, set my alarm, and get ready for bed. When I wake in the morning, I'm relieved to see messages from my friends.

Nova: You're forgiven, you little gremlin. We all know I can't resist a dirty martini.

Ivy: Let's do Chance? They have a great happy hour... We can start early!

Kenny: As long as we eat too. I won't be able to hang if we don't eat.

Nova: We'll eat! We'll drink! Let's just be merry!

Kenny: Meet there at 5 p.m.?

Ivy: Can we make it 6? I've got a hair appointment...

Nova: DO NOT get your hair blown out for drinks. Then, you'll look better than me...

Ivy: I always look better than you, biotch. But it's highlights!

Nova: Ooh! Blonde or caramel?

Ivy: Caramel.

Nova: I love! So jelly right now.

Kenny: Can't wait to see it, Ivy!

Ivy: Allegra, you in?

I reply instantly.

Me: I'm so in! Can't wait to see your new hair, Ives! And yes, happy hour at Chance at 6. XO

Nova: YAY! I'm so excited! We needed a girls' night like yesterday.

Me: Truth. Friday!!

Placing down my phone, I move to shower and dress for

the day. But there's a bounce in my step and a lightness in my soul.

Dex was right. Making things right with my friends is most important. Already, I feel better than I have in days. In fact, I can't wait until Friday night with my girls.

Hopefully, they can take my mind off Derek.

EIGHT

DEREK

"WE'RE CRASHING Allegra's happy hour on Friday night," Mav informs me.

I glance up from the lyrics I'm working on. "How'd you swing that? Does she know I'm coming?"

"She doesn't know I'm coming," he replies, walking into my kitchen and swiping a can of Pringles. Popping the top, he grabs a handful of chips. "Her friends invited me."

I narrow my eyes. "Her friends?"

Mav chews loudly, crumbs tumbling to the floor the cleaner mopped an hour ago. Fucking Mav. While Levi, Jameson, and I all bought houses, or in my case, a condo, in cities around the country, Mav still couch surfs like a college kid who can't afford decent beer. "Yep. They like me; I'm charming." He grins, his blue eyes gleaming.

"Whatever. What time? And where?" I stuff my lyrics into a binder and stand from the couch.

"Place called Chance. Six p.m."

"Sweet." I smack him on the back. "Thanks for hooking that up."

"I'm hoping I can get a hookup out of the arrangement

too. Have you seen A's friends?" He whistles. "Fucking smoke shows."

I snort and swipe my keys off the kitchen counter. "Nah, haven't met any of them yet. I'm going to run some errands. Need anything?"

Mav gives me a look. "Stop stalking her."

"I'm not—"

"Go." He points to the door. "I don't want to hear your dumb excuses."

I chuckle and head for the door. Before I leave, I tug on a baseball cap. I don't know if the hats conceal my identity, but I continue to wear them when I'm out in town.

Settling behind the wheel of my ride, I drive down to the NGO Allegra volunteers at. As much as I want to disagree with Maverick, I can't.

I am following Allegra. I'm worried as fuck about her, and I hate that I know nothing about her life here. She's the busiest college undergrad I've ever known, juggling work and extracurriculars and friendships the way most college kids juggle beer pong tourneys.

I park my car—a nondescript Toyota Camry I use to get about when I'm trying to blend in—near the entrance to the NGO. It's next to a large park, and moments after I arrive, I spot her.

Allegra, with her shocking blonde hair and her tight-ass jeans, sashays over to a group of homeless guys. They check her out hard but don't make a move to touch her. She says something and a few of them chuckle. One of them points to something in the distance. Allegra pops that sexy hip and places her hand on it, drawing another guy's attention.

I sigh. Fuck. I hate how accessible she is, simultaneously out in the open yet all alone. Still, I'm proud of her for finding something she cares about and sticking with it. From the start of last summer, Allegra had her heart set on social justice initiatives and community engagement. It's nice to know that she carried that back to LA with her and it wasn't a one-summer thing.

I look around the area, noting how seedy it is. The asphalt is cracked, with weeds growing. The space it littered with squashed Coke cans, used condoms, and the occasional needle.

Does she come here at night? Alone and vulnerable?

Does she carry Mace or a whistle on her keyring?

Does she think of consequences before flinging herself, idealistic and delusional, into environments like this one?

My jaw tightens and a sourness coats my stomach as I consider all the awful things that can happen, at any time, to any woman. It's not something I ever considered before and as I watch Allegra interact with the group of men, the feelings coursing through me pull me up short.

Did I expect Allegra to come back to California and fall into the life she left behind? Yes, I did.

I didn't expect her to forge a new path, one with dangerous side effects and unforeseen issues.

One of the guys slings an arm around her shoulders and she doesn't recoil, doesn't shake him off. Whether it's because she doesn't want to hurt his feelings or because she truly doesn't mind his touch, I don't know.

I don't know anything about her anymore.

And it bothers me a hell of a lot more than I thought it would.

A text beeps on my phone.

Mav: Hey! Jess is doing the paperwork so we can visit Levi as soon as he's cleared to see us. Most likely in a month. Maybe A will want to come?

I toss the phone on the passenger seat, not bothering to respond.

Levi. Allegra. Right now, I don't understand what either of them is doing with their lives. For years, I was the one fucking up, stepping out, making mistakes. Now, two people I care about more than most—the Rousell siblings—have become strangers when I've always considered them steadfast.

Friday night, at happy hour, I'll remind Allegra what we once had. What we can be, together. I'll show her that I'm not giving up on us, the way I stupidly did in August. I'll prove that this time, I'm capable of being the man she needs.

The guy she wants.

The one she first fell for.

MY WEEK PASSES QUICKLY as Johan tosses some tasks on my plate. Between work, keeping tabs on Allegra, and getting pulled into Mav's social circle, Friday's happy hour is a welcomed reprieve.

I dress in ripped jeans, a fitted black T-shirt, and fancy kicks for the laid-back vibe. Mav raises an eyebrow when he spots my sneakers, but he doesn't comment.

"Alfred lined up a driver for the weekend," he says, referring to our driver in Boston. "Security too."

"Thanks for organizing everything, Mav," I say, realizing just how much shit he's sorted for me, and the other guys in the band, over the last week. Hell, the entire time we were on tour.

Mav stops short, giving me a wide-eyed look. "Yeah. It's no problem."

His obvious surprise makes me feel worse. Over the past

few months, since Allegra, and tour, and Levi checking into rehab, it's dawned on me that I'm not as tuned in as I should be. Not with my surroundings, or my friends, or life in general.

I love the music. I breathe the notes and bleed the lyrics. I've been doing it for so damn long that I've mentally checked out of parts of my life that require attention and care.

Fucking consideration and common decency.

I grip the back of my neck and pinch the skin. Throw Maverick a bone I should've tossed his way years ago. "Want to work on some lyrics this weekend?"

He straightens, his eyes studying me. "Yeah. Sure." He plays it cool but the excitement that flickers through his eyes, the way the corner of his mouth curls into an almost-smile lets me know it's important to him.

"Sweet," I agree.

"Come on, we don't want to be late. Your Cinderella may leave with another prince if—"

"Shut up," I cut him off.

Mav snickers as he pulls the door closed behind him. We slip into the back seat of a black Suburban, exchange greetings with the driver, and talk about music until we arrive at Chance.

A flicker of unease rolls through me as I follow Mav into the packed space. I keep my head down, ignoring the whispers of my and Mav's names, pretending the cameras pointed in our direction aren't there. Our security cuts a path forward and when I look up, we're standing beside Allegra's table.

"Hey, Mav!" One of Allegra's friends waves.

"Ladies." Mav grins his irresistible smirk, dialing up the charm. He wraps an arm around Allegra's back and presses a kiss to her temple. "A. Introduce us to your friends." He's hilarious, keeping up the pretense of needing an introduction, when it's obvious he's already connected with Allegra's girls.

Allegra huffs, her glare cutting to me for a breath, before she turns her gaze, considerably less annoyed, back to Mav. "Seems you already know them."

Mav and one of the women laugh.

"Nope. Just me!" The laughing woman raises her hand. Ah, she's the friend Mav must have reached out to.

"I'm Nova, this is Ivy, and"—Nova points out the women at the table—"Kenny." She taps a woman with strawberry-blonde hair and unsettling blue eyes.

"Kenny?" Mav quirks an eyebrow.

"Mckenna," Mckenna clarifies, her eyes narrowed as they take in Mav.

I stifle a laugh. Mckenna may be the only woman I've ever seen not instantly eat up Mav's charm. A fellow skeptic. I like her already.

"Hey. I'm Derek." I shuffle forward to introduce myself to the table.

All four women stare at me for a long moment, their expressions ranging from curiosity to dislike to outright hostility.

Damn, tough crowd.

"All right!" Mav claps his hands together. "How 'bout a round of shots?"

All four women swing their gazes—and smiles, save for Kenny—toward Mav.

"Tequila would be great," Ivy concludes.

Mav signals for a server who swoops toward our hightop. I squeeze my way in between Allegra and Nova, hooking my elbows onto the table ledge. Mav orders shots, I tack on a beer, and the girls ask for another round of cocktails.

"Allegra was just telling us how she managed to get off work tonight," Nova says, easing into a group conversation.

"We'll come visit you one of these Fridays," Ivy promises. "Beirut is always a good fucking time." She glances at Mav. "Have you guys been?"

Mav shakes his head. "No, it's a club?"

"More like a lounge," Nova tosses out. "But Allegra makes good money there so it's more of a professional than student scene."

Beirut. The lounge where she serves.

"You work weekends too?" I blurt out, my tone more hostile than I would have liked.

"Gotta pay the bills, Reign," Allegra tosses back.

Nova bites her bottom lip to keep from laughing.

"When do you study?" Mav wonders.

"She doesn't," Mckenna answers, her tone serious.

Allegra rolls her eyes. "I'm doing fine in my classes. Why is everyone ganging up on me? This is happy hour; it's supposed to be fun."

"A's right," Nova agrees, rushing to her friend's rescue. "TGIF!" She lifts her mojito glass and juts it toward the center of the table. "And we're reunited."

The girls follow suit, so Mav and I clink our glasses as well. We all take long sips, the levity easing some of the tension now hovering over the table.

"Allegra!" a voice calls out.

I turn and sneer when I see—

"Ethan!" Allegra lifts a hand in greeting. "I'm glad you could make it!"

"When did you invite Ethan Dresden?" Nova asks.

"When did you invite Mav and Derek?" Allegra shoots back.

Nova's face falls at Allegra's sharp tone, and Allegra dips her head, embarrassed. "We had coffee this week after class, and I mentioned it to him." Her eyes dart around the table. "It's cool, right?"

"Of course," Kenny says soothingly.

Not at all.

Mav shoots me a warning look. I drain my fucking beer.

Ethan reaches our table and pulls Allegra into a hug. He says what's up to the other girls before saying hey to Mav and flipping his chin at me. I can tell he can't stand me but that's fine, I don't like him either.

"How'd your exam go, babe?" he asks Allegra like they're a fucking couple.

I narrow my eyes. Are they?

"Fine. Good." Allegra flicks a wrist, turning more into his frame. "I passed so, that's all that counts, right?"

No one, not even Ethan, replies. Allegra was a stickler where her grades were concerned. It's something I remember about her from when she was in fucking high school.

"Don't stress it," Ethan says finally. "One poor exam won't mess with your GPA."

Allegra shrugs like she doesn't care either way.

Her friends exchange a worried look that clues me in just how out of behavior her new outlook is.

"Let's get you a drink," Allegra says, glancing around for a server. She flags one over.

Her eyes dart around the table nervously, taking in her friends, me, Mav, and Ethan. She smiles but it's forced. "Let's party!"

Everyone takes a gulp of their beverages but I'm not sure if it's in agreement or apprehension.

Either way, I order more shots and another beer. Tonight's off to a rocky start and I can already tell it's going to head downhill from here.

NINE
ALLEGRA

THE SECOND SHOT of tequila goes down easier than the first. As the alcohol burns a path down my throat and into my stomach, I release a shaky exhale.

Why the hell are Mav and Derek here? And why did Ethan have to show? I told him about happy hour as an off-handed comment. When he mentioned passing by, I couldn't tell him not to come, but I didn't think he'd show up.

I glance at my friends. Girls' happy hour is going sideways. I wanted to hang out with my friends tonight. Confide in them about Derek being in town, about Dex stepping in as a solid mentor in my life, about the two people I placed in housing this week.

I wanted to hear about their lives. Talk more about Ivy's new haircut and ask Nova if she's been on any dates. See if Kenny heard back from the law schools she's applied to.

Now, all those conversations have been paused. Instead, we need to make nice and entertain the three guys surrounding our table, giving each other dagger eyes.

Well, mostly Derek is glaring at everyone but that's nothing new. He never knew how to have fun, enjoy a moment for what it is, and make friends. He's too busy being sour and judgmental, snarky and self-centered.

"I need another shot," I announce, giving myself up to the moment.

Why the hell should I tiptoe around this male pissing contest? Besides, my friends invited Mav and Derek here; they can deal with the bullshit their presence is causing.

Me? I'm going to enjoy my Friday night off.

When the server passes our table, I order another round of shots.

Happy hour slides into night and Chance fills up. College kids, young professionals looking to blow off steam, and groups of friends line the bar and huddle around the high-top tables.

The DJ arrives and tipsy cliques of girls flock to the dance floor, their laughter genuine, their friendships tight. I watch them move and glance at my friends.

"Want to dance?" I ask the group but look at Nova since she's the more carefree of my friends.

"Sure." She slips off her barstool.

I slide off mine and stumble slightly. Derek places a steadying hand on my lower back, his eyes catching mine.

"You good?" His voice is low. Gravelly. His eyes are dark and intense. Two pools of coal I used to drown in. Hell, maybe I did drown in them and still haven't come up for air.

My breath lodges in my throat and I nod since words fail me.

Derek dips his head, brushing his lips over my ear. "You sure?"

I turn my head and ignore him. Why is he questioning me? Why does he feel entitled to a response?

I follow Nova toward the dance floor. She grips my hand and weaves us through gyrating couples and dancing bodies. Pulling us into the center of the dance floor, we move to the music. Ivy eventually joins us.

A mash-up song plays and when I hear the opening notes of The Burnt Clovers' hottest single, my eyes cut to the table.

Mav fist pumps, enjoying the song and the energy it's creating. Ethan's nowhere to be found. And Derek? He's staring at me with pure hunger and unadulterated want.

My body comes alive under his intense gaze. Heat spreads up my spine and fans out through my limbs. My nipples pebble, pressing into the cups of my bra. A rush of desire gathers between my legs.

Fuck. I turn away from Derek.

Why does he do this to me? Why is he here?

Why does he affect me more than any other man in my life? Still, after all the fucking heartache he caused?

Angry with my traitorous body and frustrated with how this night is going, I close my eyes and focus on the music. Blocking out the lyrics, I lose myself to the beat. My arms lift in the air, and I swivel my hips seductively. I sense bodies moving closer; their heat presses into my skin.

A steady frame steps behind me, one hand possessively grabbing my hip. For half a heartbeat, I hope it's Derek but as soon as the guy's cologne hits my nostrils, I know it's not. His touch is different. It feels wrong and sloppy. Still, I sink into his hold, letting him guide our dancing. When he presses a pill into my palm, I don't think twice. I swallow it dry, opening my eyes long enough to see the rage that crosses Derek's expression.

In the next instant, my angry rockstar is before me, slapping the guy's hand off my hip. Derek gives him a menacing look and the guy takes off without a word. I don't even know his name. In fact, I don't even know what he looks like. And yet, I took a pill he passed me.

"Are you out of your fucking mind?" Derek snaps. He grips my wrist and tugs me away from my friends and off the dance floor.

When we get back to our table, he sits me on a barstool and steps between my parted knees. His palm, surprisingly gentle given the currents of anger in his eyes, rests against my cheek.

"Look at me, Allegra," he demands.

I fight to open my eyes. Fuck, I'm tired. The club spins around me, the lights blinding, the sounds drumming in my pulse. Whatever I took is dragging me under.

"Baby," Derek mutters, his voice scratchy. Panic replaces the anger in his eyes. "Fuck. Is this a goddamn habit?" he bites out accusingly.

A shiver runs up my spine. Anticipation—or maybe expectation?—travels through my veins. I like that he cares. I smile. I want him to worry. Hell, I've worried about him for way too long.

"Shit," Ethan says behind him. My new friend gathers my hair in his fist and pulls it over my shoulders. Ethan's fingers press in the center of my back. "Want me to take you home, A?"

"I'll be taking her home," Derek snaps.

"Hey, man. Take it easy." Ethan's voice sounds dull compared to Derek's threatening one. Ethan gives me a little shake. "Allegra?"

Derek's face fills my line of vision. "We're leaving." I

feel his hands move down my body and then, everything is upside down as he flips me over his shoulder.

"You can't just—" Ethan sputters.

"Get the fuck out of my way," Derek cuts him off. "Mav? I got her. We're leaving. Get the girls home."

I don't hear Mav's response. Instead, I focus on not vomiting. Or passing out. Or drifting off to sleep right here, with Derek carrying me through throngs of people.

I'm sure these images will appear in tabloids tomorrow morning. At least I'm wearing sexy underwear. The thought makes me giggle and Derek's palm massages the back of my bare upper thigh in response.

I guess because he's Reign, no one puts up a protest to him carrying a blitzed girl out of a club. Or perhaps his security clears a path for him. Whatever the reason, it's mere minutes before cool air races over my heated skin and I know we're outside.

"Come on," he says gently, turning me right side up.

The world rushes past me quickly and my stomach recoils, threatening to upchuck all the shit I consumed.

Derek sets me in the back seat of an SUV. He brushes my hair out of my eyes and looks me over with a searching, concerned gaze. Then, he pulls the seat belt across my chest and buckles me in before rounding the car and sliding in beside me.

He rattles off my address to the driver. Of course, he knows where I live.

The driver takes off in the direction of my house.

"Here." Derek uncaps a water bottle and holds it to my mouth. "Drink this."

At his words, I realize how parched I am. I do as he says and greedily drain the water bottle.

"Good girl," he murmurs.

I snort. I was his good girl once.

Now? I'm too fucking damaged to be anyone's good anything.

"Allegra," Derek murmurs my name.

I drag my eyes open and look at him.

His expression is filled with sadness and lined with regret. "What are you doing, baby?"

I smile softly and let my eyes close.

Living my life. Having fun. Being a college kid.

The responses filter through my mind, but I don't voice any of them. I'm too tired to talk. Too tired to navigate whatever is happening between Derek and me.

Exhaustion weighs down my limbs. My tongue feels too thick for my mouth. My throat, tight and sore.

The next thing I know, Derek's cradling me in his arms and working his way into my apartment. He finds my keys in my purse and lets us into my studio. Placing me down gently on the couch, I hear him move around my space.

"Fucking shithole. Living like this." The deadbolt slides into place. A kitchen cabinet opens. Followed by the refrigerator. "No food, no Advil—"

"In the bathroom," I croak out.

Derek's sigh fills the air.

I don't know how much time passes before he presses two tablets into my mouth. The rim of a glass knocks against my teeth. "Drink," he commands. One of his hands cups the base of my head, holding me up enough to swallow the cool water. I drink, swallow, flop back, and close my eyes.

Derek carries me to my bed. He lays me down in the center and pulls off my heels. He unzips my skirt and works it over my hips. Then, he pulls the sheet around my waist.

His fingers work through my hair. The bed dips as he

sits on the edge. His scent envelops me, and I breathe it in, letting his presence soothe me.

For so long, this is all I wanted. Him. His attention, his care, his *love*.

"You left me," I murmur, accusingly.

"Biggest regret of my fucking life."

I snort. Good. I'm glad he regrets it. He should.

"You're killing me, baby," he whispers.

My eyes are closed, my breathing even, my mind half numb. But I hear his words. They filter into my subconscious and knock around like a ping-pong ball.

"Hate seeing you like this." Another stroke of his hand passes over my head. "I thought I was doing you a favor, but if I knew it would be like this..." he sighs heavily. "Fuck, Allegra. What the hell are you doing, baby?" His mouth moves over my cheek. His lips brush a kiss to the corner of my mouth. "I love you, Stellina. So much it fucking hurts."

I love you.

He's never said the words before. And now, he says them when I'm too incoherent to respond. Hell, maybe I'm imagining them? Dreaming them up and willing them into reality.

Still, his words heal some broken part of my heart. Mentally, I promise myself that I'll talk to him about this tomorrow. I swear that I'll confront him, ask him why he thought abandoning me was good for me, try to understand his thought process like a rational, mature adult.

But when the morning light cuts through the curtains and I wake up, disoriented, groggy, and hungover as hell, I don't remember a damn thing Derek said in the quiet of the night.

"You shouldn't be here," I tell him instead, right before I

race to the bathroom and empty the contents swimming around my gut.

"Tough shit," he replies, standing in the doorframe of my bathroom, witnessing my humiliation, my shame and desperation.

His presence ignites my anger all over again.

TEN

DEREK

Good. So am I.

Standing in her bathroom's doorway, seeing her, on her goddamn knees, her skimpy shirt from last night twisted, I want to shake her. Her eyes are rimmed in red, her hair a tangled clump at the base of her neck, her face lined with creases from her pillow.

Still, she's fucking gorgeous. My cock stirs for her, timing be damned.

I clear my throat. "You can't keep living like this."

Her eyes flash, hot anger streaked with a defensive edge. "Like what?" She rises on shaky legs. Her palms press into the bathroom vanity, anchoring her, as her head swings in my direction. "Like a normal, twenty-two-year-old college kid who pays her own way in life?" She tilts her head, glances at the ceiling as if it will provide her with knowledge. Or patience. "Hm." She taps her bottom lip. "My bad for not making it big with a record label and swimming in millions by now."

Fucking dramatic. "That's not what I meant, and you know it."

She rolls her eyes and jams a toothbrush into her mouth. Flipping on the faucet, she cleans her teeth, ignoring my gaze in the mirror's reflection. Sighing, I give her a few minutes to pull herself together.

I retreat to the kitchen and check out her cupboards, relieved she has the good sense to stock coffee. I slept like shit on her crappy couch. A strange passage of time spent checking on Allegra, fighting my concern for her well-being, and debating the best way to announce that she's moving out of this hellhole.

She enters the kitchen and I pass her a mug of coffee.

She takes it between both hands and blows on the brew. "Thank you."

I tilt my head toward her small, round kitchen table. "Sit."

She rolls her eyes but takes a seat. I take the chair across from her and swallow a long sip of my coffee. "Last night, that a habit? You regularly take pills from fucking strangers?"

She shrugs one shoulder. A bare shoulder with the thin strap of her tank already hanging off. My fingers curl into a fist. I want to reach out, tug the damn shirt clear off her sexy body, and lay her out on this fucking table.

I close my eyes and try to pull my mind out of the damn gutter. This isn't the time for that, and I know it. Fuck, I'm worried as hell about my Stellina. But even now, she tempts me. I want to soak up her innocence as much as I want to devour her sass.

"You gotta be smarter than that, Allegra." I gentle my tone, wanting her to really hear me. "You didn't even know that guy who passed you that pill. It could've been laced or—"

"I know. It was stupid," she cuts me off. Her voice is small and her shoulders slump. "I fucked up."

"You've got solid girls in your corner. Why're you blowing them off?"

"Been busy."

I raise an eyebrow.

"I work, remember?" she taunts.

"Yeah. You're breaking your ass to live like this." I stretch an arm wide to encompass her shitty apartment.

"I—"

"I'm not saying it to be a dick. And I'm not trying to embarrass you or make you feel bad about the life you're providing for yourself," I interject, before our civil conversation devolves into name-calling. "It's admirable, how hard you work. You're a fucking hustler, Allegra. Badass. But you've got something that most people in your shoes don't."

She leans back in her chair and crosses her arms over her chest, waiting.

"Friends. People who adore you. Who fucking lo—"

"Don't say it," her voice breaks.

Yeah. She's right. Saying the L word right now would rip both our scabbed-over wounds wide open. I said it last night and I'm not sure if I'm relieved or pissed that she doesn't remember this morning. "We're gonna look at apartments today."

Allegra straightens quickly. Her chest knocks into the edge of the table and some of her coffee splashes over the rim. "I'm not a charity case, Derek."

"Never said you were."

"Why are you doing this? Getting involved in my life? I

obviously mean nothing to you, so why are you fucking here?" Anger threads through her tone but it's the pain underneath that squeezes my heart. I hate that I did this to her. That my foolish fucking actions twisted her up so damn badly.

"You mean everything to me," I admit, my voice hard. Honest.

She scoffs.

I reach over the table and grasp her wrist. "I'm done entertaining your shit. It's not safe here, Allegra. You can hate my fucking guts, but I won't have you putting yourself in these dangerous, messed-up situations."

"Right, because you live like a saint!"

I ignore her. "I already contacted my real estate agent. She's lined up three places for us to check out. They're not luxury penthouses so don't get too excited; they're neat, normal apartments in *safe* areas. Pick one without flipping me your attitude, and I'll help you pack."

She pulls her arm back and glares at me.

I take a sip of my coffee, waiting for her reaction. No doubt, an outburst.

The Allegra from summer would've discussed this like a calm, rational woman. This version is all over the damn map, keeping me on my toes and surprising me at every turn.

"Fine," she says finally.

I raise my eyebrows, not expecting her to agree.

She stands and takes her coffee cup with her. "If you want to blow your money on a summer fling, go for it. I know you can afford it and I know this little act of chivalry is more about you appeasing your fucking guilt than it is about me." She leans closer to me, a smile that doesn't reach her eyes curling the corners of her mouth. "But trust me, this act of gallantry won't help you sleep easier, Reign. It's too late for that shit."

She spins on her heel and strides from the kitchen. A moment later, I hear the shower turn on.

"Jesus," I mutter, running a hand over my hair.

I pull out my phone and tap out a few texts. The first confirms the meeting place and time with my real estate agent. Next, I let Mav know Allegra is moving.

Pulling up my email, I roll my eyes at another fucking message from my agent, Jess, letting me know that my so-called long-lost father, Derek Madden, has reached out via his lawyer yet again.

Why won't this guy take a fucking hint? One, he's most likely not my father. Two, I want nothing to do with him either way.

Are you sure you won't hear him out? Jess's words annoy me. Why is she pushing this so hard? Derek Madden started contacting me a little over a year ago. Does he think persistence will get me to crack?

No. I type out the response and press send.

"I'm ready," Allegra announces, standing in the entrance to the kitchen.

I look up at her and almost smile. Right now, with her damp, wavy hair, fresh-face, and dressed in cut-off jeans and a simple T-shirt, she looks like the girl who flipped my world upside down last summer. Minus the blonde hair.

"Let's go," I say, standing up. I rinse my coffee mug out in her sink and grab my keys. "I need to swing by my place to rinse off and change. We're meeting the real estate agent in an hour. If you're hungry, you can eat while I change."

"I'm fine," she replies.

I frown. Is she so low on funds that she's not eating? I give her a once-over as she waits for me to leave her studio.

She's thinner than she was over the summer. Frailer. Her hearty glow has dissipated into a strung-out brittleness.

"We'll get lunch afterwards," I decide. She's gonna fucking eat something in my presence today, even if I have to shove it down her throat.

"I have work."

I smirk at her. "We can hit a drive-thru. Come on."

She kicks the toe of her sneaker against the floor, ignoring me. A moment later, she follows me out and locks up.

Not that it would matter. An amateur could break into her place in under a minute. But...that's why it's moving day.

Even if Allegra doesn't know it yet.

ELEVEN

ALLEGRA

I SNOOP through Derek's stuff while he's in the shower. His condo is different than I imagined it would be. I'm used to the worn-in and well-loved look of the Boston brownstone.

Derek's LA unit is contemporary and bright. Immaculate and tidy. For sure, he has a cleaner or housekeeper, but still, this place is a more polished, grown-up version than the band's headquarters.

"What're you doing?" Mav's voice cuts through my thoughts.

I gasp and close the closet door. "You scared me, Mav."

He snorts. "Snooping, were you?"

"I didn't know Derek had an LA place." I cross my arms over my chest, refusing to apologize like common decency dictates.

Mav smirks. "Derek has a lot of things he doesn't talk about."

"Like his whiskey label?"

Mav nods. "Exactly. I hear you're going house hunting."

I roll my eyes. "Derek's making a big deal out of nothing."

"Popping pills at a club with strangers isn't nothing, A."

I close my eyes. "It was a mistake."

"See you don't make it again."

I open my eyes. "That's it?"

He shrugs. "Who am I to judge?"

"Exactly. Thank you." I gesture toward the closed bathroom door. "Derek's on a fucking high horse acting like—"

"He's worried about you," Mav cuts me off. "We all are." He points to my shirt and when I look down, his finger runs up my face to tap me on the nose.

I grip his finger and tug. "Smart ass."

Mav chuckles. "I'm serious though. You've changed."

"Yeah, well, having your brother, the guy you just fucked, and one of your best friends abandon you without a word, would change a girl, ya know?" I try to sound blasé. Unaffected. But my voice trembles and Mav hears it.

His expression falls and he mutters a curse. "I had no idea, A. If I did—"

I hold up a hand to stop him. "I know. It doesn't matter now. What's in the past is the past."

"Not when it follows you, and makes waves, in your present," he counters.

I shrug. "I'm here, right? Letting Derek take me to look at apartments?"

"Yes," Mav agrees. "You're here. And I'm so damn happy to see you." My friend wraps me in an easy hug. "Pick the most expensive place; he's good for it," Mav whispers, trying to make light of the situation.

I snort. "I hate feeling like a charity case."

"Everyone does." He shrugs. "How do you think I felt all those years with my brother paying for my shit? And then afterwards, when everyone assumed Jameson was pulling my weight with the band?"

I roll my lips together, recalling the rumors Mav mentions. When The Burnt Clovers got their big break, haters were quick to point out that Maverick wouldn't have made the cut if Jameson wasn't holding it down for him. "But you proved them wrong."

He grins. "Exactly. So can you. Be better than this, A. Be safe and smart and happy. Prove him wrong."

The bathroom door opens, and Derek stands there, a towel loosely wrapped around his waist.

I check him out so hard I'm surprised my eyes don't get stuck.

Droplets of water travel down his hard chest, pooling in the ridges of his well-defined abs. My throat dries and my nether regions clench. His hair is slicked back, made darker by the water, and a two-day old stubble gives him an edgier than usual vibe. He's naked, save for the thick black ring he wears on his left middle finger, and the ink that crawls up his arms and scrawls across his chest.

Mav sighs and points at me. "That's my cue." He moves toward the exit. "Hope you find an apartment."

"She will," Derek replies. He leans against the door-jamb and lifts an amused eyebrow. "What're you doing in my room?"

"Snooping through your shit," I admit.

He smirks. "Find anything good."

"Yeah. Your *Playgirl* collection is weak sauce. Shouldn't you have outgrown that by fifteen?" I gesture toward the pile of dirty magazines he has stacked in the corner of his bedroom.

Derek laughs. "That's a stupid prank Mav and Levi played on me last year."

My expression falls at the mention of my brother's name and Derek catches it.

"You talk to him?" he asks.

I shake my head. "He hasn't contacted me so..."

"He's not allowed outside contact for a few more weeks."

"Oh." Glad Derek knows more about Levi's life than me. "Well, my parents haven't reached out either so..." As far as Mom and Dad are concerned, Levi and I have both turned out to be such massive disappointments, we might as well be dead. At least then, they could openly mourn our loss in their community.

"Mav and I are going to see him as soon as he's cleared for visitors." Derek watches me closely. "You can come...if you want."

I look around his room, trying to sort out how I feel about his offer. Do I want to see Levi? What the hell would I even say? Does he want to see me? Does he even care about me?

"Think about it," Derek says, letting me off the hook. "No pressure."

"All right."

A beat of silence extends between us.

Then, "Do you mind?" He points toward the door.

I snort. "You don't have anything I haven't seen before."

"You better be talking about seeing me naked and not some other fucking chump," he tosses back, dropping his towel.

Fuck. My eyes snap shut.

Derek laughs.

I slowly crack my eyes open as he strides to his dresser, all confident swagger. His dick swings between his legs, long and as big as I recall. I can't help but check him out because I'm a mere mortal who hasn't had meaningful, sober sex since Derek. Since summer. Since the night he told me I was his everything.

Was that a lie?

No matter what happens, just know that the way I feel for you, it's real.

I blink away the memory. Swallow back the emotions it evokes.

Derek pulls on a pair of boxer briefs and ripped jeans. He dons his signature black T-shirt and a black baseball cap.

"Ready?" he asks.

I nod and move past him, out of his bedroom, and toward the front door. A few minutes later, we're riding in his Toyota Camry and I finally relax.

I like that it's simple, just me and him. No security, no intimidating black SUV with tinted windows, no driver.

I reach over and fiddle with his sound system, opting for the radio instead of a curated playlist.

One of The Burnt Clovers' songs comes on and Derek reaches out. He changes the station.

I snort. "Not a fan?"

He grins at me. "Pick your favorite song. What are you listening to lately?"

"Nothing by you guys," I admit. My voice is harder than I intend and Derek winces. A flicker of remorse works through my chest, but I don't apologize. Instead, I search through my iPhone and play "Numb Little Bug" by Em Beihold.

Derek listens to the lyrics, a curious expression crossing his face. "Is that how you feel? That life's too exhausting and you're barely making it?"

I shrug and glance out the window. "Mostly, I'm numb," I admit to the passing landscape.

Derek's quiet and I turn to look at him.

"Except when you're around," I continue. "I feel…"

"What?" He looks at me, his eyes dark.

"Fucking furious."

He nods, his palm slipping over the top of the steering wheel. "But that's better than feeling nothing, right?"

"I haven't decided."

Derek sighs and reaches over. His hand finds mine and he grasps my fingers. He holds them tightly, so I can't shake him off. But the truth is, I don't want to.

For this stretch of time, these minutes of simplicity, it feels nice to have someone hold part of my broken. To keep me from bleeding out.

To remind me that I can still feel things. Give of myself. Even when I think I'm empty.

"GOOD TO SEE YOU AGAIN, DEREK," the real estate agent, a woman in her fifties with bleached blonde hair and blue eyeshadow, greets us.

She's one of the first women—in any age group—to not gawk at Derek and I instantly like her. She's got this funky, throwback vibe going on and it works.

"You must be Allegra." She shakes my hand.

"It's nice to meet you." I manage a smile.

"Thanks for doing this on short notice, Deb," Derek says.

Deb waves a hand. "Of course. I've got three places to show you. This first option is the largest and most expensive."

She pauses, her gaze darting between Derek and me. Derek shakes his head and Deb glosses over the price, launching into the rental's details instead. "It's got an adorable balcony with access to a community pool and grilling pits. Come on."

I follow her up the stairs and into the apartment. It's a beautiful, breezy two-bedroom unit that is so far out of my budget, it may as well be a luxury penthouse.

"What do you think?" Derek asks.

"I think this is way too much," I say gently, trying to be appreciative.

"It's not," he retorts.

"Well, I don't *need* a two-bedroom," I add. "Unless I get a roommate." I pause, worrying my bottom lip. "Ethan mentioned—"

"We're ready for option two, Deb," Derek cuts me off.

I stifle a chuckle and follow Derek and Deb out of the apartment.

Option two is perfect. I fall in love with it the moment I enter. It's a simple, one-bedroom apartment with an open-concept floor plan and high ceilings. Big windows give the space a lot of natural light. The kitchen is newly remodeled with dark countertops and white cabinetry.

"I love it," I murmur, running my palm over the cute kitchen island that houses two barstools.

Derek grins. "Really?"

"Really," I say, biting my bottom lip. "But Derek, I—"

"She likes this one, Deb." He turns toward Deb.

"Excellent! This space also has a community pool, although it's smaller than the last one. No grills but you're closer to the town center, only two blocks from a plethora of restaurants and coffee bars."

I turn in a circle in the living room. "It's got an...energy about it."

Derek scoffs. "No need to sage the space, Allegra."

Deb chuckles. "Want to see the third option?"

"Sure," I agree. If option three is decent and significantly less money, I'll opt for it.

As much as I appreciate Derek's concern and what he's doing for me, I hate the thought of him—my ex-hookup—paying for my lifestyle. It makes me feel...cheap, even though I know Derek's reasons, deep down, are noble.

Not that I'll tell him that.

Option three is decent and less money. I sigh, knowing it's the practical choice even though my heart is set on number two.

"I'll give you a few minutes," Deb says, stepping into the hallway to give us privacy.

"You like the second one," Derek announces, correctly reading my expression.

"This place is perfect!" I reply.

Derek grins. "Allegra, I want you to be happy. And safe. And secure. I want you to pick whichever place makes you feel all those things. This isn't charity. This isn't anything but a friend helping out someone he cares about who is doing her damnedest to make things work. Don't read into it and neither will I."

I bite the corner of my mouth. "The first one is too expensive."

"Dammit, Allegra," he sighs, narrowing his eyes. "Do you know how much money I earn? I'm not trying to be an asshole here, but I can buy any of these places and would think about it as much as buying you lunch from a drive-thru."

I scoff. Imagine having that much money? That type of security?

"Pick one," he enunciates his words.

I exhale. "I like option two the best."

Derek smiles. A real smile that lightens his eyes and gives a glimmer of the playful personality he keeps on lock. It's my favorite version of him.

A pang cuts through my chest and I look away.

"Good. Me too," he agrees. "Deb, we've got a winner!" He moves toward the door to make the final arrangements with Deb.

I grin, feeling a lightness replace some of the heavy hurt I've been carrying around since coming back to LA.

These past few months, I've stretched myself thin. While I'm not looking for a handout, Derek's generosity takes a huge weight off my shoulders.

He reenters the space. "Lunch?"

I nod. "But it's on me."

"Alle—"

"Please, Derek. Let me get lunch." I place my hand on his arm. "Thank you for all of this. I can't... It means a lot to have someone, to have you, look out for me like this."

His eyes blaze, a complicated swirl of emotions, and he dips his head in reluctant acceptance.

"I'll drop you at work after we eat," he says softly.

"That would be great."

We leave the apartment together, waving to Deb as we turn toward Derek's Camry.

For a moment, I let myself imagine what it would be like if we were a normal couple. Just a guy and a girl wildly in love, picking out our first apartment, going to lunch to discuss moving in together.

I glance at Derek. Note his larger-than-life presence and the way people passing us by do double takes, looking at him for long moments with recognition flaring in their eyes.

No one approaches him for a photo, but I know that's more luck than anything else.

No, a guy like Derek will never live a simple, normal life. And a girl like me isn't destined for anything else.

We had no shot from the start.

TWELVE
DEREK

"THANKS FOR YOUR HELP." I toss Mav the keys to the truck he borrowed.

"For A? Anytime," he replies easily. "Catch you later." Mav slides into the driver's seat and pulls away from Allegra's old place.

She's almost done with her shift at Beirut and tonight, she won't be sleeping here. Taking in the shape of the building, the boarded-up windows and sagging porch, it's hard to imagine Allegra called this place home for the past few months.

I wonder what Levi would think if he could see his sister. The old Levi, the guy I first met, before The Burnt Clovers blew up, before the fame and the women and the fast pace of our lives, would be appalled. That guy would've moved his sister overnight. He would've shown up with pizza and beer and asked her what she wants out of life, volunteered himself and his network to help her achieve her dreams.

The Levi of last summer barely made time for his sister. He was too busy snorting coke and fucking Allegra's high school frenemy behind her back. Is he horrified by his behavior now? Does the guilt eat his stomach like acid during the late nights? When he can't sleep, does he regret not taking the olive branch when Allegra extended it?

Does he wish he could back to the start of summer? To the beginning of our tour? Do it all differently?

Fuck, I wish I could.

I kick a rock onto the unkempt lawn and turn away from Allegra's old rental. Good fucking riddance.

Getting into my car, I point it toward Beirut and wait for Allegra to finish work.

While I wait, I fiddle with my phone. Another email from Jess. This fucking Derek Madden won't quit.

Blowing out a sigh, I tap on the attachment to open the letter from Madden's lawyer.

Scanning it quickly, I slow down to reread one portion.

Mr. Madden wasn't aware of his son's birth, or that he even had a child, until Judy Reiner's death when Derek Reiner was twenty-five-years old. Shortly thereafter, Mr. Madden checked into a rehabilitation center and began...

Judy Reiner's death.

My mother was fucking dead, and no one bothered to tell me. How the hell did I not know? She passed after the band blew up, and yet, she never reached out.

Was it an overdose? Was it an illness? Why the fuck would Derek Madden know before me? He was a guy she fucked, and I was her goddamn son.

A strange sensation flows through my body, gathers in the pit of my stomach. I stare through the windshield, at the rows of parked cars, and try to recall her face. The sound of her laughter. The scent of her perfume.

Squinting, I drag up an ancient memory, the edges faded like an old photograph. Like even my mind can't bear to recall it vividly. She was beautiful, for a brief time. Long, blonde hair that curled around her shoulders. She used to wear it pulled back in a navy clip. She was wearing a sundress decorated with cerulean blue and white flowers. She was barefoot, chasing me around the kitchen in a game of tag.

"I'm gonna get you!" she taunted.

I squealed, running as fast as my legs would carry me. I misjudged my distance from the countertop as I cut the corner and caught the side of my forehead, right above my temple, on the corner.

My sob cut the air and my mother—Judy—scooped me into her arms, bringing me to her chest. "Oh, Derek," she sighed. "Let's clean you up."

The smell of antiseptic wafted around me. Her gentle touch as she placed a Band-Aid on the cut. The streams of sunshine in the kitchen. Her bare feet.

I shake my head and the memory fades.

I chuckle but the backs of my eyes burn. I press my thumb against the small scar that's hidden by my hair. One memory; I found it. One moment of happiness with my mom before the stints in the shelter started, before child services got involved, before the foster system bullshit and Simon's rough hands.

But I have one good memory. And even that ended with bloodshed.

I blink a few times, trying to clear the moisture that gathers in my eyes.

"Fuck," I mutter, tapping the end of my fist on the top of the steering wheel. "Pull your shit together, Reign. She was a goddamn drug addict."

But she was your mother, my mind replies.

I blow out a shaky exhale, relieved that the back door to

Beirut opens and Allegra steps out. Her presence, even through the windshield, soothes me. Helps me push away the confusing thoughts about my mom, about my childhood. I open the car door and step out, keeping the door between us.

She smirks when she sees me, and it warms my heart.

A smirk is better than a middle finger.

"What are you doing here?" she calls out, walking toward me. "I lined up a ride with a girl I work with."

"Wanted to take you home, to your new place." I toss her keys.

She catches them easily, glancing down at the key ring, her finger tracing the whistle I added in addition to her new keys, before meeting my eyes. "Just like that? It's that easy?"

"Your old landlord has been paid until the end of the month. I got your security deposit back." I hold out an envelope with some folded-up bills.

She regards it and hesitates.

"Take it, Allegra." I push it closer.

She finally relents and takes the envelope, slipping it into her back pocket. "Thanks."

"Let me take you home," I say.

She shakes her head. "I've gotta sleep at my old place tonight. Pack up and—"

"You've already been moved in," I inform her.

Her mouth drops open, and she places a hand on her hip. "Derek, you can't just—"

"I already did. Come on." I tilt my head toward the passenger seat.

Allegra huffs out a sigh but walks around the front of my car and slides into the passenger seat. I sit down and flip the ignition, turning the car toward her new place.

"How was work?" I glance at her.

"Busy." She taps out a text on her phone and sends it.

"You tired?"

She stifles a yawn. "Yeah." She looks at me and her eyebrows knit together. "You okay?"

She notices. She knows. That stupid swell of emotion rises again. This time it crashes at the base of my throat, and I clear it, nodding.

"All good," I say, unable to stop my grin. I glance at her, and my smile widens. She cares.

She narrows her eyes. "Why are you looking at me like that?"

"Like what?" I chuckle.

She points at me. "Stop smiling; it's fucking creepy."

I laugh and look back at the road.

In my peripheral vision, I note that Allegra rolls her eyes, but she's smiling.

For a heartbeat, it's like old times between us. There's that tug of understanding, partly from muscle memory and partly because we've still got it—the spark, the chemistry, the connection.

When we arrive, I walk her up to her new apartment and idle outside the front door.

When it swings open, she glances at me. "You coming in?"

I shake my head.

Confusion twists her expression. "Why not? I assumed this arrangement came with some...strings." Her eyes dart from me to her apartment and back again.

A beat of anger pulses through me. Is she joking? She better be. "Nope. This arrangement is to keep you safe. Comfortable." I lean over and brush a kiss to her cheek before I can check myself. "Good night, Allegra."

She watches me curiously. "Night."

I tip my head toward her open door. "Go in now and lock the door."

She nods, steps over the threshold, then closes the door and flips the deadbolt.

Once I hear it slide into place, I let out a deep exhale and return to my car. Then, I drive home, shoot the shit with Mav, and slide into my bed. Alone.

But for the first time in months, since summer in Boston, I don't feel lonely.

***

I GIVE Allegra space for the next few days. As she settles into her new place, I get busy with promoting River Wells Whiskey. On Saturday, I wrap up an event early after learning from Mav that Allegra is hanging in tonight.

Picking up some Italian takeout, I take my chances and drive to her place.

"Still stalking me?" she asks when she answers the door. But one side of her mouth tugs up and her eyes soften.

"I brought a peace offering," I reply, holding up the takeout bags.

"I thought the apartment was the peace offering," she mutters as I step inside her place.

I walk into the living room and look around, liking the homey touches she added. Her couch, as uncomfortable as it is, looks better in this space. A simple throw blanket rests over one side. She even hung two pictures and added some knickknacks.

"Looks good in here," I comment.

I set the bags down on the kitchen table. Allegra grabs two plates and utensil sets from the kitchen and places them on the table. "Wine?" she asks.

I smirk. "I hope I can keep up with you."

She chuckles and moves back to the kitchen. A moment later, she returns with a bottle of red wine tucked under her arm and two filled glasses. She passes me one.

"Cheers, Derek," she says.

The sound of my name in her voice—the soft, sultry tone—sends goosebumps over my arms.

"Cheers," I reply, clinking her glass before taking a sip. "This is decent." I smack my lips.

"I've got good taste," she reminds me, sitting down at the table and reaching into the brown paper bag.

Once our plates are filled, she points at me with the tines of her fork. "So, what are you doing here?"

"Just came to hang out."

"How'd you know I was home? And alone?" She lifts an eyebrow.

I sneer at her "alone" comment. She better not be bringing any fuckers, like Ethan, around. "Mav."

"Traitor," she mutters.

We eat in silence for a few minutes.

Then, she looks up again and stares at me.

"What?" I ask.

"Why are you being so nice to me? I mean, over the summer, you messed with my head every chance you got. You ran so hot and cold, you gave me whiplash. And now, you're..."

"I'm what?" I place my fork down, wanting to hear what she has to say.

"You're present. Looking out for me, showing up for me, being...I don't know, *nice.*"

"I always looked out for you." I scowl at the insinuation that I didn't, even though I understand her point. "I just did it behind the scenes."

"Exactly. Why are you all...front and center now?"

"Because doing it the way I was hurt you," I say honestly.

She rears back, surprised by my candidness.

"Allegra, I know I fucked up. I know my leaving hurt you. But I truly thought it was for your own good. Fuck, baby, I resisted you all damn summer. You're Levi's sister and Levi was hanging on by a goddamn thread. You've got this bright future ahead of you and the band was heading out for a full European tour. If you came, if we fucked around and it didn't work out... I was worried that it would affect the band, Levi, and hurt you. Instead, everything I hoped to avoid came true and it was infinitely worse than I could have imagined."

"With my brother?"

I nod. Sigh. Grip the side of my neck. "Yeah. Levi was in rough shape." I look up, catch her dark eyes and hold them. "And you. I had no idea you..." I roll my lips together. Give her the truth and hope she's ready to hear it. Accept it. Forgive me for it. "I'm sorry, Allegra. I'm sorry for hurting you. I'm sorry for leaving you. And I'm sorry for making you doubt me."

"I never doubted you," she says softly. "I doubted *me*. My ability to judge someone's character. My ability to hold on to a good thing... I'm no longer angry with you, Derek. But I don't trust you."

"Yeah, that's fair," I say, meaning it. I wouldn't fucking trust me either. "But I'm going to win back that trust, Allegra. I swear it."

She snorts and twirls spaghetti on the tines of her fork. "Good luck."

"I don't need luck."

She looks up again.

"I'm persistent as hell when I go after what I want. And I've wanted you from the first time I saw you."

She stares at me for a long beat before raising her wine glass and taking a sip. When she looks back at her plate, she breaks the moment.

I take a sip of my wine and focus on eating dinner, on enjoying the presence of her company for what it is.

A moment with my Stellina.

THIRTEEN

ALLEGRA

"YOU'VE GOT NO SHOT," I tell him as I deal him his cards.

"This game is better with more people," he says.

"Be quiet. Everyone loves Uno."

"I didn't say I don't like it. I just said—"

"I heard you," I cut him off. "I'll go first."

"Shocker," he mutters.

I grin and place down a red seven.

Derek drops a red nine.

A random rerun of *Friends* plays in background. We sit around the coffee table, drinking wine, and playing Uno for two rounds.

"I won again!" I hold a hand in the air.

"How do you know I didn't let you win?" Derek challenges.

"Pfft. You're too egotistical to allow someone to beat you. I have a better strategy."

"Strategy?" He snorts. "It's Uno, not chess."

"I could beat your ass in chess too," I bluff. I don't know how to play chess.

Derek's eyes sparkle. "Next time, we'll play chess."

"Planning to make this a habit, are you?" I tease him.

"I'll take any time with you I can get, Allegra."

Well, that declaration shuts me up. I have no idea what to make of this new version of Derek. He's done a one-eighty since leaving me in his bed in late August.

Can someone really change in five or six months?

Did Levi's going to rehab affect him?

Did losing us hurt him as much as it gutted me?

I bite the corner of my bottom lip, chewing thoughtfully.

I don't trust Derek, and yet, I can't deny that since he showed up, he's been good to me. Generous. Thoughtful. All the things I wish he showed me over the summer.

I drain my wine glass and move to top up both our glasses.

"You sure, Stellina?" Derek murmurs.

I smile. "I can hold my own, Reign."

He sighs. "I hate when you call me that."

"Everyone calls you that."

"But you're not everyone. When you say it, it adds this... distance between us."

"Maybe we need distance."

He snorts. "Baby, we just had over five months apart. With the entire country and the Atlantic Ocean between us. I don't want any more fucking distance."

"How long are you staying in town?" I ask, trying to quell the flicker of hope that he could be staying. I squash it, knowing better than to trust those feelings.

"As long as it takes."

I lift an eyebrow.

"To win back your trust," he answers my silent question.

I sip my wine slowly. When I place down my glass, my tongue darts out to swipe across my upper lip.

Derek catches the movement, and his gaze darkens. Heats.

"My trust or me?" I ask, my tone huskier than it was a second ago.

"Both," he replies simply. Truthfully.

I shift closer to him, moving onto my knees.

He regards me warily but doesn't flinch. In fact, he doesn't move at all as I slide my palms up his hard chest to grip the tops of his shoulders.

"You sure you don't want quick and easy?" I taunt him, leaning closer. My mouth drops to the side of his neck, my lips grazing his earlobe. "I remember you didn't like to get your hands dirty. Nothing that takes too much work." I swipe my tongue over his hot skin.

His hands clench my hips. "Stop, Allegra."

I chuckle. Moving up, I straddle his lap. "Stop what?" I pull back to look at him. "I thought you wanted me, Derek. Isn't that why you're here?"

"Yeah," he says, his tone hard. His eyes flash. "But I want all of you, baby, not just this sexy body."

His words send a thrill up my spine. I straighten my arms off his shoulders and tilt my head, pretending to think. "Hmm, but what if I'm only offering my body? I don't trust you, remember?"

"You should only offer this body to men you trust. Fuck that," he backtracks. "Only to me."

"Take it or leave it," I mutter, our mouths lined up. My breasts drag across his chest on each inhale.

"Allegra," Derek groans, sounding tortured. His one hand finds the back of my head and his fingers thread through my hair. "Don't tease me."

"I'm not," I say softly. "I missed this with you. I want you, Derek." I roll my hips over his lap. I haven't fucked anyone since that drunken night after Beirut. I don't know if it's my changing luck, the wine I consumed, or Derek's presence, but right now, I want him to make me feel good. I want his hands to grip and touch and coax my body into submission. I want his mouth on mine. I want to burst apart at the seams, and I want to yell his name as I do it.

"Fuck, Stellina." His voice breaks. His eyelids drop to half-mast.

His cock hardens beneath me as I roll my hips again. Rocking against him, I press myself against his chest and move my lips a whisper away from his.

"Kiss me, Derek," I beg. "Remind me how good it can be."

He snaps. His lips press against mine, his hand in my hair tightens, and his other palm slides to the small of my back, pulling me closer. I arch into him, grind down on his dick, and part my lips.

Derek's tongue slips inside. He kisses me hard. Wildly and recklessly. I unleash my months of pent-up hurt and anger as well, kissing him just as desperately. Kissing him to prove a point. My resentment spills out in the bite I give his bottom lip. His loss shines through in how easily he takes it, practically begging me for more.

He rocks forward, until he gets his feet underneath him. Gently, he lays me out on my living room floor. His body covers mine as he grabs both my hands and moves them above my head.

I giggle, a reminder of that night—us getting hot and heavy against a brick wall in an alleyway behind Taps— flaring in my mind. Derek grins wickedly before kissing me again.

This time, it's slower. This time, his hands roam over my body, caressing my breasts and palming my hips. I press up into him, pulling off his shirt and popping the button on his jeans.

"Want you," I remind him, pushing his boxers off his hips.

When his cock springs free, it points straight at me like a homing beacon. Fuck. I wrap my hand around his silky-smooth skin and pump him once. Twice.

He glances down between us, pure satisfaction crossing his face. He works my leggings down my hips eagerly, giving up as soon as he can dip his hand underneath the waistband of my panties. His fingers swipe up my core and he sighs.

"Missed this," he says, popping his fingers into his mouth and sucking off my arousal. "Mm, so fucking sweet."

I shudder, my desire spiking at the visual of him tasting my want. Then, his fingers are back between my thighs, playing and coaxing. I pump him faster, tightening my hold. Our eyes meet, our chests heave, our mouths part.

Derek lunges for me, pressing his mouth against mine and knocking my hand on his cock away. Then, he's traveling down my body, ripping my panties off in the process. His face disappears between my thighs, and I cry out, arching my back as his tongue, his magical fucking tongue, latches onto my sensitive bundle of nerves.

"Derek," I pant. My one hand wraps against the leg of the coffee table and hangs on while the other finds purchase in my living room carpet. I buck against Derek's face.

In response, two of his fingers enter me. His fingers fuck me while his mouth devours me. My body tightens and coils, the pressure building until I can't take it anymore.

Squeezing my eyes shut, I cry out. "Fuck, Derek, I'm—"

I can't finish my sentence because I break apart, orgasming hard and fast as he continues to lick my core, lapping at my arousal like it's his favorite fucking dessert.

When my body goes limp, he pulls away and watches me warily.

I stare up at him.

"Christ, but you're fucking beautiful," he murmurs, his hand moving over my hair, fanned out around my head.

"Lose these." I tug on his jeans which are still around his knees.

He pauses. "Allegra, we don't have to—"

"Now," I cut him off.

"You sure about this?"

"I'm sure," I swear. Right now, I want to feel him fill me. Stretch me. Fuck me into oblivion.

At my declaration, Derek kicks his pants off quickly.

"Condoms are in my beside drawer," I say.

A rush of fury rolls over his features. "Why the fuck are—"

"Go get one; hurry!"

He swears colorfully but retrieves a condom and rolls it on. When he's back in between my legs, he braces one hand next to my head and looks down at me. "This changes things."

"Okay," I murmur.

"Tell me you want this, Stellina."

"I want this," I breathe out. "I want you."

He enters me on one, sharp thrust and I cry out, wrapping my fingers around his biceps. Derek pulls all the way out before slamming into me again. He does this a few times before we find our pace. He sets a rhythm and I catch up to it, fusing my lips to the side of his neck as he fucks me hard. Frantically.

"Yes, yes, oh God," I chant as another orgasm builds.

"Get there, baby. Fuck, get there."

I do. Finding my release, I claw at his shoulders and throw my head back. "Oh God, Derek."

He pumps into me two more times before gripping my hair and spilling inside me. "Fuck, Allegra. So goddamn good, baby."

Our chests are coated with sweat as Derek lays me back down. He stares at me for a long beat before pushing off and moving to the bathroom. He returns a moment later with a warm washcloth and runs it between my legs.

I sit up and take it from him to clean myself up.

He stares around my living room, still naked, and snorts. "Well, that escalated."

I chuckle. "Yeah. But it was good."

"Fucking great," he amends.

I nod. He reaches down a hand and I let him pull me up. "I'm going to shower." I move toward the bathroom.

"Hey." He touches my hip. I look at him. "You okay?"

"Yeah, I'm great." I tip my head toward the bathroom. "You can rinse off after me."

His eyes narrow slightly, a cloud passing through them. "Okay."

"Okay," I say.

I step into the bathroom and close the door. Turning on the shower, I wait for the steam to fill the small space before I step under the showerhead.

Then I let out a shaky exhale and sag against the tiled wall.

What the hell was that?

Shaking my head, I try to make sense of what transpired between Derek and me. Of how good he made my body feel. Of how easily he made my thoughts slow. Of how perfectly we came together.

But I can't trust him. I can't let him in.

I can't end up broken-hearted again. Especially when my heart hasn't healed from the first wounds he inflicted.

Not even a little.

"WE SHOULD TALK." The words are out of my mouth the moment she opens her eyes and I mentally berate myself for being so desperate.

Shit, I'm acting like a damn chick. Like one of the groupies I used to blow off.

But the way things ended between Allegra and me last night—a blasé good night and flicking off the lights—left me unsettled. We have too much history, too much respect, to let things go as a causal sign-off.

Allegra scrubs the sleep from her eyes and presses herself up. She looks at me, her blonde hair a wild wave around her head. "About what?"

About what? I snicker. "Seriously?"

She shrugs and collapses back to her mattress. She stares up at the ceiling before glancing at me. "It was just sex, Derek. Relax. I know it was a mistake; you know it was a mistake. We can just move on..." She sighs. She checks her fucking phone. "We don't have to overanalyze it."

"A mistake?" I repeat, dumbfounded. She thinks last

night was a mistake? "I mean, sure, it would've been better if we weren't drinking or—"

"It's no biggie." Her eyes find mine again. Warm cocoa. Sincere. "Really."

Her blasé outlook on us hooking up kicks me straight in the chest. "No biggie," I repeat again.

"I gotta get moving," Allegra says, dragging herself from bed. She stands, reaching her arms overhead to stretch, and my eyes snap to the round curve of her ass.

Last night, I had my hands all over her; this morning, I'm a no biggie mistake. Fuck, I'm not even significant enough to be an *actual* error in judgement.

I'm...nothing.

The realization sours my stomach. Frustration kicks up, rushing through my limbs like an adrenaline hit.

"Want coffee?" Allegra glances over her shoulder. Polite, civil, uninterested.

"Nah, I'm good." I stand from the chair beside her bed and rub my palms over the thighs of my jeans. "I gotta get going."

"'Kay. Thanks for hanging last night." She walks me to her door in her fucking silk panties and crop top.

She's confident and brazen. Beautiful and bold.

Infuriating as hell.

I want to remind her about last night. About how good it was. About how I said sex would change things and she said okay.

But my pride holds me back. Instead, I grunt, unable to form words.

"Have a good day," Allegra calls after me as I stride out of her apartment.

I lift a hand in farewell and hear the apartment door close.

Damn, her rejection stings. Her dismissal burns.

The fact that I don't register as more than a casual fuck —a goddamn mistake—cuts.

Is this how I made countless women feel the morning after? Hell, I didn't even offer consolation coffee.

Shaking my head, I dip into my car and drive home. Restless energy swims through my veins, electric and hyped up. Halfway to my house, I make a detour, swinging by one of my friend's music studios instead.

I knock on the door, taking a chance that he spent the night recording. He's a night owl like that, does his best work when the rest of the world is passed out.

"What's good, Reign?" Hendrix asks when he opens the door. He doesn't look surprised to see me, but then again, nothing catches him off guard.

He's a guy who goes through life with his eyes wide open, taking things as they come, and not bothering to question them one way or the other.

"I need to..." I trail off, unsure what the fuck I need.

"Create," he supplies, reading my expression. Hendrix holds the door open wider.

"Thanks, mate." I step inside.

He yawns and picks up a to-go coffee cup. "I gotta sleep for a few hours. The space is yours. You good?" he wonders.

"Straight," I say.

"Have at it," Hendrix mutters, walking through the space to a back door that leads to his personal apartment.

I sit down in the booth and grab a notebook and pen. Tapping the pen against the edge of the paper, I stare into space, recalling the lyrics that haunted me all summer. The ones I put on hold during our tour because I could never get them right.

You vanished like daybreak,

Lost stars and forgotten night.
You haunt me like a shadow,
Clingy and relentless.
You haunt me like her.

———

MY FINGERS ITCH as I jot down the lyrics. Then, my scrawl keeps going. My mind whirs, trying to keep up with the movement of my hand.

You faded like a photograph,
Broken memories and echoes of lost dreams.
You stalk me like my conscience,
Vile and futile.
You stalk me like pieces of her.

———

STARS DIE AND PLACES MERGE.

You turned my rebellion into a
Resentment that burns.
All consuming and exhausting,
You hate me like her.
No, you hate me like me.

———

I DROP my pen and reach for a guitar. Straddling a banged-up barstool, I strum out a few chords before my fingers find the rhythm. My voice is all gravel, half wounds and half regret, as the song pours out of me.

It's tortured me for the better part of this year, but I finally understand the desperation behind it.

It was Allegra all along.

Allegra and me and what was never meant to be.

I sing until my voice is hoarse and my fingertips are numb.

When I finally remove the strap of the guitar and look up, I note Hendrix in the sound booth.

He gives me a long, searching look before he slow claps a few times.

I shake my head. "It's not done."

"It is." His voice comes through the speaker.

"It's not polished," I push back.

Hendrix shakes his head. "It's not supposed to be. A song like that... It's honest and that honesty is in the rawness. It's achingly beautiful, Reign, because it's so fucking sad."

I grip the neck of the guitar for a long moment before I set it down.

"Who is she?" Hendrix asks knowingly.

I narrow my eyes at him, and he smirks, but it's not condescending. It's poignant.

"That's why it's done," he advises. "Because she still fucking haunts you. And worse? She's got you checking your own bullshit. Honest, man. Can't mess with that."

I blow out a sigh and scrub at my eyes.

"What time is it?" I ask.

"You've been here nearly four hours."

"Fuck," I mutter. "I gotta go..."

"Crash?"

"Yeah. And eat." My stomach grumbles.

Hendrix laughs. "But the music feeds your soul."

I move into the booth and nod. "Yeah. It does that." I hold out a hand and he shakes it. "Message you later?"

"Absolutely. You've got your next single right here." He

taps the top of the counter. "Whether you release it solo or with the Clovers, it's a song that deserves to be heard."

"We'll see," I say, uncomfortable with the thought of being so vulnerable.

I mean, I put myself in that position every time I write lyrics, or record, or perform on stage. But something about this song—something about Allegra Rousell—pulls me up short.

"Get some sleep, Reign."

"Yeah. Thanks again, Henny." I give him a wave before I cut out of his studio.

The sunlight assaults my eyes as I walk toward my car.

A few paps are hanging around and they scramble to snap my photo when they see me.

"Reign! Are you recording a new song?" one of them calls.

"Where are the guys? Does this mean you're finally going solo?" another shouts.

"Is The Burnt Clovers breaking up?" a third chimes in.

Fucking hell. I dip my head and beeline for my car. When I slide behind the wheel and pull out into the morning traffic, I flip the paparazzi off. Don't they have something better to do with their time?

I drive home in silence. The emotional high of bringing Allegra to climax, of wrapping her in my arms, of feeling her body move beneath mine has sunk in the reality of today.

A fucking mistake.

And yet, her words, her animosity, finally fueled the lyrics that have escaped me for months. Hendrix was right; that song is my next single. Do I bring the guys in? Do I go at it alone? Does it even matter anymore?

When I get to my place, I take a hot shower. Then, I

close the blinds, pull on some sweats, and drift off into a deep sleep.

For the rest of the week, I avoid Allegra. I don't seek her out. I don't check up on her. Instead, I lose myself in the music and it helps reestablish my equilibrium.

It feeds my fucking soul.

FIFTEEN

ALLEGRA

IT'S BEEN a week since I slept with Derek. While I tried to be chill the morning after, I think I played it too cool.

Calling him a mistake was an overreach. Now, he's not speaking to me, and Mav hasn't mentioned Derek once in the handful of times we've talked or hung out.

While work is going well and the girls and I are clicking again, there's a hole in my life. I thought I was pulling myself together, but all it took was Derek showing up in LA to light the match that burned my progress to the ground.

One night. One hot and sexy hookup and I'm back where I started.

Is he done with me? Is he thinking about me? Will I ever not be plagued by insecurities where Derek is concerned?

Sighing, I swipe on a coat of lip gloss and give myself a once-over in the mirror. I tuck my hair behind my ears and wonder, for the first time since I made the radical change, if I'm done being blonde. Maybe I should go back to my natural color? Maybe I should stop trying so hard to be something I'm not?

Shaking my head, I grab my purse and leave my place. Driving to the coffee shop to meet Ethan, I listen to some throwback tunes that make me recall my first few years of college.

Sushi dinners with Nova, Ivy, and Kenny.

The cellist I lost my virginity to.

My first pep rally.

Drinking wine coolers on hot summer nights and laughing with my friends.

Those memories seem framed in innocence now. In a sweetness I no longer possess. Is it because of Derek or me that I lost that carefree, rose-colored-glasses worldview?

Does it matter?

To be honest, I'm too tired to care. Jaded and bitter and worn down. Back then, everything was new and exciting and tinted with possibility. Adventure.

I sigh heavily as I park my car. When I enter the coffee shop, Ethan is already seated. He rises when he sees me and I wave, making my way over to him.

"You look beautiful." He kisses my cheek in greeting.

"Thanks." I smooth my hands over my short, flirty summer dress.

"I got you a latte." He gestures to my caffeinated beverage of choice.

"Perfect." I sit down across from him. "How's your week been?"

"Not bad." He waggles his eyebrows. "I had a date."

"Oh, do tell." I lean closer. Ethan and I have hung out a few times now and while I know he finds me attractive, I also know he's seeing several people. Keeping his options open.

"His name is Sam. He's a Scorpio," Ethan divulges.

"We both like soccer and baseball so there were a lot of easy topics to get things rolling."

"Put you both at ease early on."

Ethan nods. "He hasn't been with another guy before so…" He shrugs. "I didn't want him to feel pressured or rushed or anything."

"Right," I agree. "You gonna see him again?"

Ethan grins. "I think so. But, you know, it's super casual."

I nod, knowing that Ethan isn't looking for a serious commitment.

"What about you?" he asks. "How are things with the douchy rockstar?"

I snort. Ethan can't stand Derek. "We hooked up."

His face contorts. "And?"

I shrug. "I told him it was a mistake."

"Was it?"

I roll my lips together and think over his question. "I'm not sure yet. Where Derek's concerned, things are…"

"Complicated?"

"And confusing," I admit.

"Just don't let him dictate your worth, Allegra. You are beautiful and smart and talented. If you decide to get serious with a man, he needs to support that."

I smile and reach over to squeeze Ethan's hand. "Thanks, Ethan. You're a good friend."

He dips his head in acknowledgement before his eyes flit to mine. "I could be more, you know?"

I nod. "I know, but I don't think I'm capable of more without the friendship line getting blurred."

Ethan leans back and sips his coffee. "I get that. Not everyone can compartmentalize as well as me."

I smile. "No, I definitely can't. What are you doing this weekend?"

"Gonna check out a club tonight. Want to come?"

I wrinkle my nose. "I'm working but I'll message you afterwards."

"Yeah, hit me up. There's usually an after party my group migrates to. Come join us if you're not too tired."

"Thanks; I will," I agree. I mean it too.

If Derek isn't going to reach out to talk to me, then I'm going to keep living my life. Whether he likes it or not.

***

"GOOD SHIFT?" Dex asks as I lean my shoulder against the doorframe to his office.

"Yeah, tonight was lit."

He grins and clasps his hands together. "Just the way I like it."

I snort and step inside. "What are you still doing here?" I drop into the chair in front of his desk and lean back. "You're usually long gone before last call."

Dex sighs and gestures to the papers spread over his desk. "Too much damn paperwork. That's the part no one tells you about running your own business."

"That you'll spend more time behind the scenes than drinking the shift beers." I point toward the bar where a bunch of the staff are having their shift beers and talking about the funniest customers of the night.

"Exactly," Dex agrees. "You heading home or heading out?"

I shrug, thinking about Ethan's offer. A moment later, I yawn. "I think home. I'm exhausted."

"How are things going with the ex back in town?"

"Confusing," I admit.

Dex leans forward, his arms resting on his desk. "He giving you a hard time?" He raises an eyebrow.

"Besides moving me into a better apartment in a safer area?"

Dex shrugs.

"No. We haven't talked in a week, which is probably my fault."

"Why?"

"I tried to blow off what's happening between us. Make it more casual than it really is."

"Ahh." Dex clucks knowingly. "So, you're protecting yourself?"

I smirk. "Yeah. It pissed him off."

"Too fucking bad."

I laugh. "I guess. But he did mention visiting my brother in rehab. Going with me, I mean. And..." I trail off, shaking my head. I don't know how to put into words how conflicted I feel about reconnecting with Levi.

"Do you want to visit your brother?" Dex asks gently.

"For the longest time, reconnecting with him was the most important thing. I went to Boston last summer with the intention of spending time with my brother. I wanted us to be us again, you know? The past few years have been... intense. And I miss him."

"It didn't go well?"

"He blew me off. Landed in rehab." I tip my head, as if that explains everything.

"Do you believe in second chances?"

I glance at Dex, noting the dip in between his eyebrows. His question is deeper than face value and at the solemnity in his eyes, I give him the truth.

"Yes. I believe in second chances." My voice shakes slightly.

"I have a lot of regrets, Allegra," Dex admits. "I've been in rehab too."

"Really?" I sit up straighter.

Dex chuckles but it holds an edge. "Really. Like I said, I have a lot of regrets. Too many if I'm being honest. But I've never regretted giving a second chance when it was warranted. And I've always been grateful for another shot extended my way. If you think you and your brother can reestablish what you once had, especially now that he's getting help and surrounded by positive influences...well, I'd hate for you to regret not trying. Family is family forever, even when it doesn't feel like it. There's always a connection there, even when the string is weak and frayed and tenuous as hell. Don't give up on that."

I roll his words over in my mind, staring at him. For the first time since Dex stepped into my life, started giving me some tough love with a side of mentorship, I wonder about his past. About his regrets. His family and his losses.

"If you were me...?" I let the question dangle.

"At my age and knowing what I know now, I'd give him a shot," he answers instantly.

I nod, almost relieved to have someone make the decision for me. Just so I can stop thinking about it. "Okay." I stand from the chair and pick up my bag. "I'll visit him. The thing is, I'm wondering about him all the time, right? So, why not go see him for myself? See if he's changed or wants to change...then, I can stop wondering."

Dex grins. "That's another way of looking at it."

I lift a hand in farewell. "Thanks, Dex."

"Anytime, A. Get home safe."

"See ya." I wave before leaving his office.

When I pass the bar, I say good-bye to my coworkers. Luis walks me to my car and gives me a hug good-bye.

I slide behind the wheel and send off two text messages.

Me (to Ethan): Hey! I'm beat so gonna pass on tonight. Have fun!

Me (to Derek): Hey, I'll go with you to see Levi. Let me know the details.

Then, I drive home, take a hot shower, and collapse into bed.

I fall into a deep sleep and no dreams—good or bad—follow me.

"WHAT ARE YOU DOING HERE?" she asks when she opens her apartment door.

I hold up the tray with two coffees and a paper bag with bagels. "I brought bagels."

She steps back as I enter the foyer and move toward the kitchen.

"So, you just brought breakfast?" She follows me into the kitchen.

I sit down at the table, but she remains standing. Allegra crosses her arms over her chest and leans against the kitchen countertop. Her tone holds a note of skepticism and her eyes narrow.

I grin and pull out a buttered salt bagel. Breaking off a piece, I pop it into my mouth. "I got your text."

"And?" She huffs, crossing to the table and taking the seat across from mine. She reaches into the bag and plucks out an everything bagel with cream cheese. She picks at it.

"We should talk," I declare.

"I'll go see Levi," she states, taking a nibble of her bagel.

"About us," I clarify.

Allegra widens her eyes, her lips parting. "You're serious?"

"One-hundred percent." I lean closer, narrowing my eyes. I know she's about to call me out on my own bullshit, and right now, I welcome it. Fuck, I've missed her.

"I spent all summer trying to get a read on you, wanting to know how you felt about me and now...you decide we need to talk and so we're gonna talk?"

"I miss you," I blurt out.

Her mouth drops open.

I smirk. "I've missed you since I left that bed with you in it in August."

She snaps her mouth shut.

I arch an eyebrow, silently challenging her to toss me her shit.

"I don't trust you," she reminds me.

"I know and I don't care. I still want you, Allegra. And I'm gonna earn back your trust. Next issue."

"I don't want a boyfriend."

"Then we don't label it." I take a swig of coffee.

"But I'm not going to sleep with you and know that you're out, hooking up with other women."

"No other women," I say easily. I've learned my lesson; all other women, fuck, all other pussy pales in comparison to Allegra. "I don't want anyone else. I want you." I point at her. "But no other men. No fucking Ethan."

She laughs, delighted that I'm still just as jealous. "Ethan and I are friends. There's nothing there."

"He's into you."

She shrugs. "Lots of guys are into me."

She's right. "What else?"

Allegra leans back in her chair. Her blonde tresses brush over the tops of her shoulders. She regards me coolly, taking a long pull of her coffee. Then, she slouches forward again. "So, we'll hook up, not sexually see other people, and just...see what happens."

A ripple of unease moves through me, but I keep my expression blank. No, if I had my way, I'd drag her across the fucking table, put my mouth and hands all over her gorgeous body, and make her mine.

In every sense of the word.

But she's gonna buck me hard and I deserve it.

So, I shrug. "If that's what you want."

"What do you want?" she asks coyly.

I grin. "You know what I want, babe. I fucking want *you*. All of you. But I'll take whatever you're willing to give until I can prove that I'm not going anywhere. So, you wanna hook up and see how it goes? I'll be in your bed every night until you kick me out."

She's stunned for a heartbeat. Then, a grin spreads over her face. "Every night?"

I laugh. "It was good, wasn't it?"

She sighs and breaks off a bite of her bagel. "Yeah, it was good. I don't..." She pauses, takes a small bite of the bagel. "I was numb for most of the sex I had last semester."

Hearing her say it fucking scores my skin like knives. The words move through my chest like razor blades, death by a thousand fucking nicks and minuscule slices.

"I hate that for you, baby," I tell her the truth. "I fucking hate myself for it, Allegra." My eyes close and I breathe out, my nostrils flaring. My hands curl into fists and tremors of rage rumble through me. I did that to her. I hurt her so badly that she started hurting herself.

"It's—"

"Don't say fine." My eyes pop open.

She shrugs. "It is what it is. It wasn't meaningful."

I bite down hard on the inside of my cheek. I know what she's explaining. I've felt it. The reckless need to push and do fucked-up shit just to feel. Cut yourself just to see if you bleed. But that's for angry minds battling darkness, for guys like me.

Not for light and sunshine. Not for a soul like Allegra's.

"Stop looking at me like that," she murmurs.

"Like what?" My words are husky, low and gravelly and covered in a thin coat of anger.

"Like you're disappointed."

"I am," I admit. "In myself. I can't stand that I made you feel anything but cherished. I hate how I treated you. I left because I wanted to protect you. And the Clovers. And me, from all the things I felt for you. But if I knew..." I clear my throat. "I never would have left."

She shrugs with one shoulder. Her bagel is a shredded pile of tiny dough balls. "I'm glad you're back," she says finally, meeting my eyes.

"I'm not going anywhere," I promise.

"We'll see," she replies, flicking a dough ball at my face.

I swat it away and snort. "So, Levi can start seeing visitors this week. You're in?"

She nods slowly. "Yeah."

"Wednesday okay? Mav and I will swing by and pick you up. Five p.m.?"

"Sure," she agrees. "That works."

"You nervous?" I ask. I saw how hard she tried with Levi last summer. He never looked out for her the way he should've; he didn't protect her the way she needed him to.

Case in point: me. Levi should knock my teeth down my throat for the way I treated his sister, and he doesn't even know.

He still has no fucking clue.

"A little," she admits. "In my mind, he's my last bridge home. My last connection to family."

"Your parents?" I wonder, even though deep down, I know the response.

"Mom and I spoke briefly at Christmas. That's it," she sighs, sorrow heavy in the sound.

"They don't deserve you."

She smirks. "I've heard that too many times for it to be true."

"I won't lie to Levi this time," I say, wanting her to know that I'm going all in.

She rears back. "You want to tell him about..." She gestures between us.

"I know how I feel, Allegra. How you want to treat this" —I gesture between us the way she did—"is up to you. But on my side, I'm all in. And I'm not going to fake that shit in front of your brother. He's one of my best friends, my band-mate, and I should've been straight with him from the jump."

Allegra lets out a shaky exhale. "I didn't expect you to say that."

I grin. "I'm doing everything by the book this time, baby. Something bothers you, you tell me. If I can fix it, I will. I know I'm gonna mess some shit up because this is new territory for me, but I won't leave you again. I don't ever fucking want you numb, not when you make me feel everything."

Allegra stares at me like she doesn't recognize me.

My smile widens. I like that I can still catch her off guard. That I can try to be the good, deserving, stable man she needs and keep her on her toes.

"Wednesday," she murmurs.

"Five p.m.," I confirm.

"Okay," she says. In that word, I know she's giving me her acceptance.

We're going to tell Levi that we are...well, whatever we are. But it's something. It's meaningful and real and the most important relationship in my life right now.

Even more so than the Clovers.

I won't lose my Stellina again. I won't let her down. I won't disappear.

This time, I'm going to prove I'm worthy of her. To do that, everyone in my circle needs to know I'm hers, even if she's gonna play hard to get a little while longer.

Allegra can build a wall between us, but eventually, I'll scale it. Smash it. Burn it to the ground.

Eventually, she'll be mine in all the ways that matter.

She'll be mine completely.

SEVENTEEN
ALLEGRA

"YOU CAN RIDE SHOTGUN," Maverick announces, climbing out of Derek's Toyota Camry.

I laugh. I love that this is his LA ride. I love that he can still surprise me and prove how not pretentious he is, even while he's raking in millions.

"How are you?" I give Mav's cheek a kiss hello before sliding into the front seat.

"All good, boo. You?" he replies before closing the passenger door.

I wait for him to take the seat behind mine. "All good."

"You sure?" Derek asks beside me.

I glance at him and try not to drool. How is his casual so hot? Even when he doesn't try, he affects me on every level. Today, he's wearing a backwards baseball cap. A slight scruff runs along his cheeks. He's wearing ripped, distressed jeans and a smoky gray Henley. A new pair of Jordan's. Nothing about his ensemble is spectacular, and yet, he gives off an energy that has my nerves scattering and my skin heating.

I rub my palms along the thighs of my jeans. Work a swallow.

"Allegra?" Derek asks, his voice low. His whiskey eyes burn.

"Huh?" I murmur.

Mav chuckles behind me.

"You sure you're okay?" Derek repeats.

"Um, yeah. Of course," I manage, shaking my head, as my cheeks flame.

Derek snorts but reaches over and places a hand on my thigh. I move my palm on top of his and our fingers link together as he pulls away from my building.

Our long drive is mostly quiet. Save for the music set to a low volume, just our mingled breathing fills the space. We're all lost in our thoughts and memories. Did the guys think Levi would end up in rehab? Should I have seen the signs earlier? Pushed back harder? Would it have made a difference?

Will he be happy to see me? Embarrassed? Worse, ashamed?

I turn to look out the window.

For my entire childhood, Levi was my constant. The steady, unwavering person I could count on. Even when my desires weren't in line with our parents' beliefs. Even when my spirit was too rambunctious for our community.

While Mom helped cultivate my passion for social justice initiatives and Dad mentioned candidates he felt would make suitable husbands, Levi encouraged me to dream. To try. To explore and experience.

But when I worked up the courage to do that, he was too wrapped up in his own life to care. He stopped being a reliable support system. He stopped showing up for me.

And when I slipped, I fucking face-planted with no one to catch me. Only myself.

Should I have noticed his pulling away sooner? Was that the first sign I overlooked?

A flicker of guilt burns low in my gut. It mixes with threads of resentment. I don't want to resent my brother and yet, I tried. I showed up. I cared. And it hurts that he was able to discard me so easily, casually, cruelly, for a fix.

"Hey." Derek squeezes my fingers.

I look at him.

He shoots me a worried glance. "You can talk to me."

"I'm fine," I say instead. What am I going to say? I'm angry with Levi? That's hardly supportive of the guy we're all rallying around in a rehab facility.

Disappointment shudders through Derek's eyes before he snaps them back to the road. A minute later, he disentangles his hand from mine.

I feel his loss instantly. It lands like a sharp smack to my cheek, and I shift toward the window.

I don't have to share my thoughts with Derek, or anyone else, if I don't want to. The truth is, I have too many big feelings. I'm overwhelmed. Confused. Hurt. Sad. Angry.

The list is endless. I don't know how to process them, much less communicate them.

Beside me, Derek sighs.

When I look at him again, he rests his hand back on my thigh. Gives it a little, reassuring squeeze. Whether it's meant to reassure me or him, I'm not sure, but I don't brush his touch away.

Instead, I settle back in my seat, close my eyes, and wait for us to arrive at the facility.

"YOU CAME," my brother breathes out when he sees me.

His voice moves through my chest like a salve, healing emotional wounds that I've let fester.

"Levi," I say as he wraps me in a hug. A big, warm, bear type of hug that swallows me up and keeps me close.

I sigh, my eyes closing, as I rest my cheek against his chest.

God, I've missed him. This, right here, is what I wanted when I stood on the band's Boston brownstone stoop and knocked. It's many months later, but right now, I feel that sense of belonging.

I feel *home*.

"God, A, you look beautiful," my brother murmurs when he pulls back.

His eyes are shiny with emotion.

"You look good," I tell him, drinking in his appearance. He looks better than good; he looks healthy.

He chuckles and clutches his abdomen. "I've put on a few pounds."

"You needed it, mate." Derek pulls him into a one-armed hug and smacks his back.

Levi's eyes find mine over Derek's shoulder. They're clear, focused, *him*.

Relief flows through my veins. He's back. My brother is back.

The realization presses down on me, the enormity of the moment nearly steamrolling me. I didn't realize, until right now, how fearful I was. I didn't understand the hold the alcohol and drugs had on him. I couldn't comprehend his addiction. At the time, I thought he didn't want me in his life. That he didn't want *me*.

To see him now, smiling and joking, causes a swell of emotion to form at the base of my throat.

Dex was right; second chances are important. In fact, they're sacred.

Mav and Levi exchange an easy greeting.

"Come on." Levi gestures toward a balcony that leads outdoors. "We can have lunch outside."

As Mav falls into step beside my brother, Derek hangs back.

He gives me a long, searching look. I smile, loving that he's concerned about me. It feels good to have Derek acknowledge how important this moment with Levi is, and care about it. At my smile, he grins.

"You hungry?" he asks.

"I can always eat," I assure him, my voice light.

He snorts and wraps an arm around my waist. When we step outside onto the balcony, Levi shoots us a glance, his eyes narrowed as they laser in on Derek's hold on my hip.

I pretend not to notice and take in my surroundings instead. The facility Levi is staying at has gorgeous grounds, complete with a five-star restaurant. Tables dot the balcony, overlooking a lush expanse of lawn before the ocean appears.

"This is beautiful," I comment.

"It really is," my brother replies.

"Take a seat," Mav says, extending a hand.

Derek moves forward to pull out my chair.

Levi pauses, watching our exchange with interest. A spray of nerves travels over my skin. I perch on the edge of my seat as the others claim chairs, Derek beside mine.

Levi slips into the chair across from me. His eyes dart between Derek and me again as he greets our server.

We order some waters and Cokes and take a beat to scan the menu. After we place our lunch orders, Mav leans back in his chair. As if sensing the shifting energy at the table, he tries to lighten the mood. "Working on your tan, I see."

My brother glances at him and cracks a grin. "Yeah. I've been spending a lot more time outside. Joined a volleyball club."

"Volleyball?" I ask. "Remember when—"

"I tried out my freshman year of high school," Levi finishes my sentence.

I nod, already laughing.

Mav and Derek glance between us curiously.

"There was this girl Levi was trying to impress," I clarify.

"Rochelle Santoro," Levi supplies.

"And she..." I trail off, shooting my brother a look as I giggle.

"She was dared to pants me by the cheerleading team," he says, chuckling.

"And she did. During try-outs," I add.

"Right as I went up for a spike," Levi points out.

"She got him so unexpectedly!" I point at Levi.

"Except I freaking landed on top of her and—"

"She sprained her ankle." I make a face.

"Never spoke to me again," Levi concludes.

"He didn't even make the team." I shake my head.

"It was a colossal failure." Levi snorts.

"But you're playing now," I point out.

He gives me a look. We both start to laugh. It's the type of story that breaks the ice. Everyone appears a little more comfortable after that. Mav laughs, Derek cracks a joke, and our appetizers arrive.

Lunch is casual and more easygoing than I imagine. My brother shoots me warm glances throughout the meal. He briefly asks about our mom and dad but doesn't focus on them the way he used to. It's more like he was asking to be polite. Instead, he steers the conversation to my studies and inquiries about my friends.

Mav fills him in on Jameson and Amelia's on-again, off-again relationship status. Derek mentions a few Clovers updates. No one talks about how the tour was cut short. Or that Derek launched a whiskey label. Or how I'm working at Beirut.

We keep the conversation friendly and light, sticking to safe topics. Still, my brother gives Derek and me curious, searching glances on more than one occasion. I know Derek mentioned he was going to be honest with Levi, but I would prefer to avoid that topic during our first meeting. Especially when it's going so well. The last thing I want to do is rock an already shaky boat.

Once we're finished with lunch, Mav points into the distance. "Reign, want to check out the golf course with me?"

I hide my smile. Good ol' Mav giving Levi and me a moment together.

Derek turns to glance at me. His eyes narrow, silently asking if I'm okay with that. I give him an encouraging smile. Across the table, Levi looks away, his jaw tightening.

Mav and Derek stand from the table. Derek places down his napkin and dips his chin, letting me know he won't be long.

I wait for them to walk away before turning back to Levi. There are so many things I want to talk about. I want to hear about how he's doing, if he's made any friends here, if he has an end date in mind, what his plan is for afterwards. Before I can ask, he tosses out his own question.

"How serious is it?" His voice is harder than it was a

moment ago. His eyes are focused on mine, scanning my expressions for clues as to what I'm thinking.

I clear my throat. "Wh-what?"

Levi sighs and reaches across the table. He takes my fingers in his hand and squeezes. "You and Reign. How serious?"

I let out a shaky sigh. Derek's the one who wanted to broach this topic and now, where is he? Looking at a damn golf course.

"It's complicated," I reply.

Levi snorts. "It always is with Reign."

"We've had a connection for a long time," I offer.

"Since summer?" He lifts an eyebrow. "But then we went on tour and he..." He trails off, shaking his head in disbelief.

My heart thumps and my stomach clenches. He what? What did Derek do on tour? Sleep with women? Dabble in drugs? Form a harem?

My throat tightens and I focus on pulling oxygen into my lungs. I have no right to be angry, especially considering the decisions I made. Still, Levi's words cause new thoughts to form and old ones to shift.

"Since my seventeenth birthday," I supply. "There's... always been something there."

My brother's eyes narrow and he stares at me, as if he can see straight to my soul. He used to. Can he still? Do we still have that type of connection? The unbreakable bond, the steady reliability, the love that's greater than our family's circumstances?

Levi sighs heavily. "I love you, A. I know I've been a shitty brother. I know I haven't been here for you. But I care about you. You're my sister. I want to see you happy, and Reign..."

"Derek," I correct. While Clover fans and Mav regularly call Derek by his nickname, I don't recall my brother ever doing so.

"He's not for you," Levi says softly. "You deserve so much more. Better."

His words cause my chest to ache. "I care about him, Levi."

"Yeah," he agrees. "He cares about him too."

I sigh. He's not telling me anything I don't know and yet, I want to believe in this improved version of Derek. I want to give him a second chance and feel like it could work. "Listen, we don't have to talk about this right now. I'm here for you. I...I miss you, Levi. And I don't want to be estranged anymore."

"Me neither," he agrees instantly. "I never did and the only reason we were is because I didn't nurture our relationship the way I should have. I'm sorry, A. Truly."

"It's okay," I say, meaning it. I forgive Levi because I want to. Because he's my family. "You're my home, Levi. You always have been."

He drops his head and swipes at his eyes. When he looks up, I can see how much my words affect him. His showing emotion, openly and honestly, causes tears to prick my eyes too. "I love you, Allegra. I'm so happy you came today. Thank you for showing up for me, even when I don't fucking deserve it."

I laugh lightly and clutch my brother's hand. "I love you, too. When you get out of here, we should spend some real time together."

"Count on it," he agrees. "I'm not going anywhere."

I smile. I've heard that before and again, I desperately want to believe it.

"Good," I say. "That would be good."

EIGHTEEN

DEREK

"I'M JUST GOING to use the bathroom and then I'm ready," Allegra informs me as Levi walks us back toward a sitting area.

"Take your time," I murmur, watching as she moves toward the bathroom.

When I turn back, Levi glowers at me.

Fuck, I knew this would happen. He may have been smashed out of his mind all summer and barely coherent during our tour, but there's no way he would miss my intentions toward Allegra when he's sober. Bright eyed and clear minded.

"What the fuck, Reign?" His tone is low, but accusatory.

"Take it easy," Mav murmurs. He grabs Levi's elbow and pulls him into a corner.

I follow at a slower clip, reminding myself to keep my cool. This isn't the place to lash out at one of my best friends.

We sit down at a small table in the corner of the sitting

room. Conscious that other people are present, we keep our tones hushed.

But the accusation in Levi's glare is evident. "Stay away from my sister," he seethes.

"It's not like that; I care about her," I reply.

He snorts and shakes his head. "You're fucking unbelievable." He looks at Mav. "Did you know?"

Mav shrugs. "It's been a long time in the making."

Levi points at me. "You're fucking my sister, while I'm in here? You messed with her head all fucking summer when you knew I was struggling, twisted up over shit. Are you kidding me, Reign? What the fuck kind of best friend are you?"

"Hey," I snap. "That's not fair. What happens between Allegra and me isn't any of your goddamn business. I don't owe you a fucking explanation."

"Let's all take a deep breath and be mindful of our language," Mav cuts in, his eyes darting to the kids visiting their mom in the center of the room.

I ignore him. So does Levi.

"She's my sister," he reminds me.

"Yeah, you've done a real good job honoring that," I clap back.

Mav sighs and closes his eyes.

Hurt streaks across Levi's expression.

"Fuck," I say, gripping the back of my neck. "That was a low blow," I admit. "I'm—"

"Save it," Levi cuts me off. "She deserves so much fucking better than you," he says slowly, his eyes pinning mine. Disbelief and disappointment war in his expression. "If you really cared about her, you'd stay away."

"I tried that," I admit. "It didn't fucking work. The way I feel for her... I love her, Levi," I admit. Fuck. I fucking love her and I haven't even told her yet. At least, not when she's awake and coherent.

"Love?" He tips his head to the side, his voice cracking. "Give me a fucking break, Reign. You don't know the first damn thing about love. Or sacrifice. Or showing up for someone else. You're the most selfish bastard I've ever met and the fact that you could betray me like this, while I'm in here..." He pauses and digs his finger into his chest. "Well, that says it all, doesn't it?"

"Allegra's coming," Mav murmurs.

Levi looks over his shoulder and stands. "I gotta get going, anyway. Thanks for coming, Mav." He gives Mav a hug. Then, he glances at me. "Call me for Clovers business only. If it's not about the band, I don't want anything to do with you." He delivers this in a low, even tone, that scrapes through me.

I nod once, accepting his terms. I hold back as he wraps his sister in a hug. He holds her close and presses a kiss to her temple, whispers something in her ear.

I hate that I can't hear it. Is he warning her away from me? Is he going to start trouble? Does he think I'll fucking back down from his bullshit ultimatums?

I glance at Mav who is staring straight at me. I point at him. "Don't tell Allegra shit she doesn't need to know. This is band business."

Mav rolls his eyes. "You're a fucking idiot." He shakes his head. "You could've handled all of this a lot better," he tacks on, before walking toward Levi and Allegra.

I hang back as they exchange a final farewell. Then, I toss my keys in the air, catch them with my palm, and lead the way to my car.

The ride home is just as silent as the ride in. It's sad, because until Levi flipped me shit, we were getting along.

Sure, it was surface level, but after weeks of silence and months of shifting feelings, it felt good. Right. Secure.

I drop Mav off at my place. He gives me a long look before shaking his head and moving up the steps to my condo.

"You hungry?" I ask Allegra.

She shakes her head.

When I reach for her hand, she doesn't stop me but laces our fingers together. Her touch allows me to breathe easier. It centers me and reassures me that we're doing the right thing.

That I'm capable of doing right by her.

That I can be enough. I can show up. I can be the man she needs.

I just need to prove it. To her, to Mav, to fucking Levi.

"He'll come around," I murmur, more to myself than Allegra.

"Yeah," she agrees lightly.

I'm not sure if either of us believes our own bullshit, but saying it out loud, and together, gives me a sense of relief.

I take her home. When I enter the space behind her, she turns toward me. I deadbolt her door and reach for her.

Our mouths clash together, edged in need. My hands grip her waist as her fingers twist in the fabric of my shirt. She moves my Henley over my head as I pop the button on her jeans. We're naked in a matter of minutes and I thank every fucking deity in existence for gifting me this beauty. For giving me a North Star.

"Stellina," I groan as she drops to her knees in front of me.

My hand finds her head as she takes me in her mouth. I'm already rock hard and wanting. She drags her tongue down the shaft of my length before sucking the tip.

"Christ," I swear, glancing at the ceiling.

Allegra works me over so fucking good, I see stars. But I just want to see her. Before she gets carried away, I pull her up and kiss her hard on the mouth.

"Want to play all night with you," I tell her.

She grins saucily. Taking my hand, she leads me to her bedroom.

She drops back on her bed and props herself up on her elbows, giving me a daring look. I laugh and straddle her hips. My fingers move through her blonde tresses.

"I like this color," I tell her honestly.

She tilts her head. "Better than me being a brunette?"

I study her closely. The lovely shape of her face. The slender column of her neck. Her deep, soulful eyes, and perfect rosebud lips.

"No," I say. "I like your natural color more. But you look hot as fuck like this too."

She snorts as I push her back and land on top of her. Then, I frame her face between my hands and kiss her. Our mouths move in tandem, a secret language where only the two of us know the words. We come together beautifully, half song, half prayer.

I bring Allegra over the peak twice before I allow myself to finish. Afterwards, I wrap her in my arms and hold her against my chest. Our hearts beat in rhythm and our fingers link together. She holds our joined hands against her hips as her back presses into my chest.

"You think he'll accept us?" she whispers finally. I know it's been on her mind. How could it not? Levi's always been her home.

"Eventually," I murmur, hoping I'm right. He has to come around, right? For the sake of the band? For the sake of Allegra?

She shifts in my arms and finds my gaze. God, I want to drown in her chocolate eyes. "You're really going to stay, right?"

She breaks my heart. I bring my face closer to hers, until our noses brush. "I'm staying right here, love," I promise. Then, I kiss her again.

She turns fully in my arms and my hands clasp her back, bring her even closer. I deepen our kiss. She mewls as her legs wrap around mine. In moments, I begin to harden against her thigh.

I thrust my hips, dragging my shaft along her silky skin. Allegra moans and the sound causes my heart rate to double. She shifts, pushing me onto my back and moving on top. Taking my cock in her hand, she grips me tightly and pumps three times before lining us up and dragging the head through her slick folds.

"You want to go again?" I taunt.

A wicked gleam lights her eyes as she grins. "Always," she murmurs, before sinking down on my length.

"Fuck, baby," I swear, loving how she takes my cock. Like we're a perfect fucking fit.

Allegra slides up and down, setting the pace, taking it how she wants it. As she gets into it, she throws her head back, arches her chest, and moans. Fuck, she's gorgeous. I love watching her take what she wants, move how she wants, reach for the release the way she likes it.

I move one hand between her legs to play with her clit while my other hand rolls over her breast. As she writhes and moans, my cock twitches inside her.

Please, let her come first, I silently pray.

Knowing I won't be able to hold on much longer, I pinch her clit and nipple at the same time. Allegra calls out my name and shatters on my cock.

"Fuck, you're so damn hot," I tell her. Before she fully recovers, I grab both her hips and thrust up into her two times before I spill inside.

And...shit. We forgot a fucking condom. For the first time in my life, I don't care. I stare in awe as my semen leaks down, over her inner thighs.

"So goddamn sexy," I swear, swiping it up and dragging it over her nipple. Her eyes are hooded and heated as they latch onto mine.

"You're fucking everything," I tell her.

"And this is real," she murmurs, reminding me of the words I said over the summer.

They hit me hard, causing regret and emotion to battle in my sternum. "Always real, Stellina," I promise.

I pull her forward and she collapses against my chest. Her breasts and thighs rub against me, spreading our mixed arousal. We're making a mess, but I don't give a shit.

Instead, I kiss her and pour my reassurances down her throat until she swallows every last sacred promise.

"This is real."

NINETEEN
ALLEGRA

OVER THE NEXT TWO WEEKS, I spend my days on campus, hanging with my friends. My evenings take place downtown at the NGO or visiting my brother. My nights are for Beirut and my shifts. But my sleeping hours? Those are spent wrapped in Derek's embrace.

My mornings begin with his lips on mine, or with his head between my thighs, coaxing me to greet the day. At night, my sleep kicks in after the high of a mind-blowing orgasm, expertly delivered by Derek's skillful fingers and mouth and incomparable cock.

Basically, I'm living in bliss. Waltzing along cloud nine.

"Someone got the D last night," Nova comments when I sit down at the table.

"Here." Kenny passes me a caramel latte I seldom purchase given the price. But it's one of my favorites.

I grin at my friends. "Correct," I tell Nova who snorts and claps. "And thank you." I give Kenny a side hug.

"What'd I miss?" Ivy asks, taking the seat beside mine.

"Your girl's blissed out." Nova points at me. "And I got a date tonight!" She shimmies her shoulders.

"You do?" I lean forward. "With who?"

"A football player." She lowers her voice. "There's speculation that he's going to get drafted."

"Damn, girl," Ivy mutters. "I'm having no luck in the collegiate athlete pool."

"You should come to his next game with me," Nova decides.

Mckenna sighs. "How do you guys have time to date? I'm drowning in—"

"Don't say schoolwork," Nova cuts her off. "Kenny, it's our senior year."

"Yeah." Ivy nods in agreement. "No one is gonna fail you."

"You guys, she's going to law school!" I remind them.

Mckenna shrugs. "I just hope I can keep up."

"You will," I say reassuringly.

"Talking about keeping up..." Nova raises her eyebrow. "You and Reign?"

I laugh. "Things are...good. We've got a good thing going at the moment and I don't want to mess with that."

"How would you mess with it?" Kenny asks.

I sigh. "Levi is *not* a fan. He keeps telling me that I shouldn't trust Derek, that I'm making a mistake, that he's not the guy I think he is."

"Who do you think he is?" Kenny presses.

"How is Levi?" Nova wonders.

"Just, worthy of a second chance," I respond to Kenny first. "I mean, he—"

"Really hurt you," Mckenna reminds me.

Ivy nods thoughtfully. "You were gutted."

"You got a blonde bob. Although now it's more lob, which suits you better." Nova points at me as if my choice of hairstyle settles just how devastated I was. Rock freaking bottom.

"Yes, I remember," I remind her. "But since he's been back, he's done nothing but show up for me. I mean, the apartment." I widen my eyes at my friends.

"And the hot sex," Nova mutters.

"Just, keep it casual," Ivy advises. "I think your current outlook is a good one. You're clearly having fun with him and there's something more there but no need to rush it or label it or whatever. Not unless you trust him?" She raises a skeptical eyebrow.

I pause. Chewing my bottom lip, I think over her question. I don't trust Derek with the blind faith I had before last summer. Maybe that was silly of me though. It was naïve. Now, I know better.

Still, a part of me wants to trust Derek. I want to place my faith in him and know, without a doubt, that he's got my back. That he cares for me. That he loves me. Could he ever truly love me?

I heave out a sigh. "I like where we're at right now."

"Good," Kenny says, her tone clipped. "And Levi?"

I smile. "He's my brother again. The old Levi. Our conversations are interesting and funny and he's not shying away from the hard stuff either. We've talked more about Mom and Dad and our upbringing. He's admitted how checked out he was last summer and how shitty he treated me, and the band. I mean, there's a lot to unpack but we're getting there. The only distancing topic between us right now is Derek."

Ivy sighs. "That's hard."

"Yeah," I agree. "Levi's my family. He's my...home."

"You've wanted to mend your relationship with him for years," Ivy points out.

"Since we met you freshman year," Nova recalls.

"I won't jeopardize that. Not when he's putting in the work to prove that he cares about our relationship as much as I do," I say slowly.

"Even if he throws down the gauntlet?" Nova wrinkles her nose.

I look at her, confused.

"Gives you an ultimatum," she clarifies.

"What?" I sputter, running a hand through my hair. "Like...him or Derek?"

My friends stare at me, but no one offers a rebuttal.

I sigh. Snort. "No, no, I don't think he'd do that."

"I hope not," Ivy murmurs.

I shake my head again and steer the conversation back to Nova and the football player.

But her words stick with me.

Would Levi give me an ultimatum? Would Derek?

And who would I choose? Which relationship can I count on?

The fact that I don't know unsettles me as much as my wanting to believe in both.

Can any woman really have her cake and eat it too? Or will we always hang suspended between our love and our family, our heart divided in two, our emotions a swirling mess of love and obligation, desire and commitment.

<hr>

"HEY, BABY," he greets me when I open the front door.

With one word, one smirk, one step forward, Derek's presence eats up the air in my apartment. His energy expands and my attraction to him activates. I rush him like a schoolgirl. Throwing my arms around his neck, I kiss him hard.

Between the conversation with my friends and my visit with Levi, I want Derek desperately. I want him to have his way with me and show me, with his body, through our chemistry, how well-suited we are. How good things are going. I want him to remind me that I made the right choice by letting him in again. By giving my body up to his nimble hands, by encouraging his tongue to invade my mouth.

"Whoa, slow down." He laughs, catching me around the waist as I wrap my legs around his hips. "What's the rush?"

"Missed you," I murmur.

One side of his mouth tics up. "Me too. Are you hungry?" He palms my ass before setting me back on my feet. "Or we could go out for a drink?"

I tilt my head. "Now? Why go out when we can stay here? Get busy..." My eyes dart to my bedroom.

Derek's eyes darken and he presses his lips together. Jamming his hands into the pockets of his jeans, he shrugs. "I don't know. Could be nice to get out, do something together. Hang."

I freeze. "What? Like...a date?"

Derek's quiet for a long moment. His eyes search mine. His jawline hardens and the muscle underneath his right eye twitches. "Yeah," he breathes out. "I want to take you on a date, Allegra. I want to do this"—he gestures between us—"with you."

"We're already doing it," I remind him, grinning cheekily.

He snorts but doesn't smile. "Why don't you want to go out with me?"

"Why are you trying to make this more than...this?" I

gesture around my apartment. What's wrong with late nights and hot sex? With slowly letting down our walls and talking? Why isn't that enough?

"Because I want more than this. I want more than just your body and your hot mouth. I want to spend time with you. And talk about things. Real things."

"We talk," I sound defensive.

"Sometimes," he agrees. He cocks his head. "You deflect a lot."

I sigh and toss a hand in the air. "Now, you're going to analyze me?"

"It's just an observation. I want to know more about your work with the NGO and the homelessness placements. You haven't mentioned much about your friends, or your visits with Levi, or—"

"Is this about Levi?" I cut in.

"What?"

"Is this because Levi and you aren't talking? Are you trying to prove something?"

"Like what?" He looks truly lost. I should back down; I should stop my line of thinking and definitely not turn it into a line of questioning.

Even if he throws down the gauntlet? Nova's words roll through my mind. What if Derek offers me an ultimatum instead of Levi?

"Do you want me to choose between you and my brother?" I blurt out, internally wincing the second I do. I'm making this worse; I'm making an issue out of thin fucking air.

Derek rears back. A flash of hurt cuts through his eyes before he shakes his head in disbelief. "Is that what you think? You think I'd try to fuck with your family shit when I know how important it is to you? Hell, when I have no fucking family to speak of?" He chuckles humorlessly. "I watched you all damn summer, Allegra. Witnessed you fight for Levi's attention, saw your face fucking crumble when he blew you off. Hated that your mom wouldn't meet you for a damn lunch. Or that your dad wouldn't take your calls."

Embarrassment rolls through me at his reminders. Followed by humiliation. Then, the burn of shame.

"You think I'd want to pit you between me and your brother, my best damn friend?" he asks, his voice low. "Fuck, you really don't trust me."

"It's not—"

"Forget it," he interjects. "You told me as much. I just thought, the last two weeks..." He grips the back of his neck. "I hoped your opinion of me was changing."

"I—" I sigh, take a deep breath, and let it out slowly. I'm not going to apologize for being confused, or wary. But, "Let's go out and get a drink. Let's...hang."

Derek snorts. "What? Now?"

I shrug. "Why not?"

"'Cause you just flipped the fucking switch on me."

"I'm flipping it back." I stand straighter, challenging him to dare me. I know I flipped him bullshit. But so has he. I'm not apologizing for how I feel, for the fears I have, but I can acknowledge that tossing them in his face wasn't fair. So... "I'll buy the first round."

Now, he laughs. "Get out of here. I'll take you for a fucking drink, Stellina."

A flicker of relief shoots through me when he uses my nickname. He's not holding a grudge.

"I'd like that," I say sincerely.

Derek rolls his eyes. "Go get dressed."

I grin. "I'll be ready in ten."

"Yeah. See how simple this could've been?" he calls after me.

I ignore his question and change into tight black jeans and a ruby red halter top. I slip on some nude heels and grab a purse.

When I step out of my bedroom, Derek drinks me in. "You're gorgeous, Allegra. Still burning too fucking hot and bright."

I smile and walk over to him.

When I get close, his arm darts out. He pulls me against his chest and kisses my lips. The kiss holds an edge, as if he's trying to convince me that this is real. Or remind himself that it means something true. His hand grabs a handful of my ass and I drag my chest across his as I arch up into him.

He pulls back to stare at me for a long moment. I don't blink or break eye contact. Instead, I drown in his whiskey eyes and wonder if Derek Reiner is salvation or sin.

"Come on." He taps my ass.

I lace my fingers with his and let him whisk me out on a date. We hit a popular wine bar and sit at the bar, talking about real things, until it's nearly 2 a.m.

Then, Derek takes me home, lays me down, and works my body over. We come together passionately, a beautiful song of desire. Our joining is a steady drum roll of touches and kisses that intensifies into a soul-baring crescendo. My body shatters for him and he gives me all that vulnerability he hides from the world. He gives me Derek, the man behind Reign.

With his arms around my naked body, my eyes flutter closed.

Tomorrow, I promise myself, *we'll talk. I'll be open and honest with him. I'll give him the words I've been denying him.*

But when I wake in the morning, his side of the bed is empty.

Once again, he's already gone.

TWENTY

DEREK

"THAT SOUNDS GOOD, MATE," Hendrix says as I play the final chord to the song.

"The lyrics aren't right," I disagree.

Hendrix shakes his head. "You're a perfectionist."

I shrug and hang up the guitar. I'm nearly there; I know I am. This song that's haunted me for months is proving to be the most complicated, and important, thing I've ever written. I have to get it right. The feeling of embodying the essence, the spirit, of what I want to convey grips me, leaving me unsettled and restless when I can't pin it down.

I slip into the room where Hendrix sits, surrounded by equipment. He takes a swig of his coffee. "That why're you up so early? Needing to get things perfect?"

"Couldn't sleep." I give him as much truth as I'm willing to share. Even though last night with Allegra was fun, she's still holding back. Yeah, we drank wine and laughed. We talked about serious topics, and I understand that she's fearful of losing her brother, of jeopardizing that relationship when she's just getting it back. The sex was fucking fire and the sound of her moans is a soundtrack I want to listen to on repeat.

But that distance still lingers. She won't give herself up to me the way I want, the way I know she's capable of. Again, I fucking hate myself for hurting her so deeply, for rattling her confidence to the degree I did.

Unable to sleep, I slipped out early this morning and forced an unhappy Hendrix to open his studio for me. At least he stuck around and provided some feedback.

Not that it's enough.

"It's getting there," I say, tipping my head toward the sound booth.

"Most musicians would reckon it's there," he volleys back.

I flip my chin. "I'm not most musicians."

"Nope," he agrees, popping the *p*. "You, Reign, are definitely not. What've you got going on the rest of the day?"

"Some work, some errands..." I shrug. I'm gonna stop by to see Levi, see if we can settle some shit between us. Partly, it's because of our history. We built the Clovers and for years, he was my closest friend, save for Dre. Partly, it's for the band. I gotta squash shit before it threatens to shake the foundation of our group. And partly it's for Allegra. I don't want her to feel torn. And the fact that she thought I'd date her just to make her choose me fucked with my head.

I want my little star to shine, not burn out and die.

"Swing by later. I got some ideas for your song. A couple of local guys I think you'll like are rolling through. An impromptu jam sesh could be good for you. Help you work out the knots." He taps his temple.

I heave out a sigh. It's been ages since I jammed for the hell of it. Just for fun. "Yeah, all right. I'll come through."

Hendrix and I exchange a bro handshake before I cut

out of the studio. I shoot off a text to Allegra, letting her know things came up with work. Then, I drive across town to meet with Johan.

Johan and I spend the morning together, going through marketing materials for River Wells. Our marketing conversation gives way to a whiskey tasting, which devolves into a late lunch.

"Come on, it's one round," Johan tries to convince me to a game of fucking golf.

"Dude, it's almost 3 p.m.," I remind him.

"So?" He shakes his head at me. "You got plans? A hot date?"

I snort even as Allegra cuts through my mind. I gesture to my ripped jeans and white T-shirt. "Do I look like a guy who belongs on a golf course?"

Johan raises a pale eyebrow. "You look like a guy who belongs wherever the fuck he says he does."

I toss my head back and laugh. "Fair, you fucker." I toss an arm around his neck and squeeze. "Have fun with your game. I gotta cut out. Got shit to do."

Johan slaps my back and I release my hold.

After I leave him, I drive out to the rehab facility. I know Mav and Allegra have been visiting Levi, but I haven't been back since that first day. Since he told me not to contact him unless it's about the band. I could spin this shit about the Clovers if necessary. But it's really about his sister, and if he cares half as much as he says he does, then he should sit down and speak with me, face-to-face. He should show up for her, the way I am.

I sit in the parking lot. Take a deep breath. Run my fingers through my hair.

My stomach feels off and my fingers tap out a restless beat on the steering wheel. I'm jumpy.

Fuck, what the hell am I nervous about? It's Levi. My best mate. A member of the band. My roommate.

I drop my head back against the headrest.

Allegra's brother. Does he know how things went south between us before the tour? Did Mav tell him? Did Allegra?

I heave out another sigh.

"Grow a fucking set," I scold myself. Then, I get out of the car and enter the facility.

At reception, a pleasant-looking woman with a bright smile greets me.

"Welcome, who are you here to visit with?" she asks.

I clear my throat and shove a hand in my pocket. "Levi Rousell."

"And you are?"

"Derek Reiner."

She nods, her eyes not giving away the flicker of recognition I'm used to. That puts me at ease and my shoulders relax.

See? You can do this. This is going to be fine.

"I'm so sorry." She glances up, genuine remorse in her expression. "You're not on the list of approved guests for Mr. Rousell. If you'd like, you may give him a call to see if he'd like to see you?" She gestures to a white phone on the other end of the reception area.

I bark out a laugh. A fucking cackle.

Is Levi shitting me? He's not going to see me. No, he didn't even add me to his stupid fucking list.

"No problem," I tell the woman. I move toward the phone but at the last second, I detour.

I'm not playing this stupid game. I showed up; I tried. Let Allegra figure out exactly who her brother is without my needing to smooth shit over. Levi doesn't want to talk? We won't fucking talk.

I step back into the late afternoon and jog to my car. Slamming the door behind me, I punch the center of my steering wheel. A short, obnoxious beep rings out.

"Fuck," I mutter, dropping my head back and turning it along the headrest. What a mess. What a fucking disaster.

Remorse sits heavy on my chest. Is this what Levi and I've come to? Is this the end of a friendship that felt more like a brotherhood to me?

I can't believe he won't see me. Or talk to me. Or treat me like a damn adult.

Pulling out my phone, I dial Dre. It rings a few times before cutting to voicemail. I end the call and move to toss my phone into the cupholder when a text rings out.

Dre: Yo! How's LA life, man? I'm tied up with some kids right now. Hit me back later this week?

I grin at the message. Dre's got his hands full with important shit—kids' futures—but still makes time for his friends. He's the real deal; he's fucking gold.

Me: Absolutely. Miss you, man.

Dre: You okay, Derek?

I laugh. Yeah, the sentimentality of my message is concerning.

Me: All good. Just thinking.

Dre: ???

Me: Head's fucked up half the time. You know how it goes.

Dre: Allegra?

Me: Her too.

Dre: She gives you an in, you take it. But only if you mean it. I'm not playing; she's good fucking people.

Me: I know. Talk soon.

I scroll through the other text messages. One from Mav,

two from Allegra, one from Jess. I sigh when I see Allegra called twice. I should hit her back and say...what? That I'm sitting in the parking lot of Levi's rehab facility, and he won't talk to me?

I shake my head, my anger rising again.

Nah, I'm not in the right headspace to talk to Allegra. I'll pick some stupid fight with her because of how twisted up I am over this shit with Levi.

Choosing the safer option to clear my head and calm down, I place the phone in the cupholder.

I like that Dre has my back but also looks out for Allegra. I like that I can message him after weeks of not talking and he instantly responds. It's a friendship I can count on, even with all the fucked-up history between us. He would understand where I'm coming from right now.

I thought I had that with Levi. I glance at the rehab facility as I flip the ignition of my car. Shaking my head, I pull out of the parking lot.

I guess not.

***

"HE'S HERE!" Hendrix welcomes me back to the studio.

"What's good?" I slap hands with him.

"Check it." He points to a few guys. "That's Jay, Skills, and Chris. This is—"

"We know Reign," Skills cuts him off. Standing, he shakes my hand. The other guys follow suit.

"Good to meet you," I say, meaning it.

"Y'all up to jam?" Hendrix asks.

Chris and Jay exchange a look. When Chris meets my gaze, he's grinning. "Hell yeah."

I laugh. "Let's do it."

We step into the booth and begin to mess around, just play random chords and covers.

Hendrix gives us feedback from time to time. But mostly, it's me and the guys playing. And then, just me, lost in my mind. The music pours through me, coming out through new lyrics and different sounds. The guys keep up as best as they can, but they're not on my level.

Still, I respect them for helping me get out of my own fucking head.

I don't know how long I play, but when I hang up my guitar, the three of them look at me in awe.

"That was something else," Chris comments.

"Fucking honor, that's what that was." Jay smacks my shoulder.

"I appreciate you," I tell them. "I needed that and... thank you."

Skills smiles. "All good, man. Hope it helped."

"More than you know," I agree.

For the first time in weeks, my head feels clearer. I expel an exhale, letting my frustration and resentment, hurt and anger, go.

Hendrix opens the door and sticks his head in. "Now, we fucking party."

The guys laugh. I dip my head, about to make an excuse and cut out, but Hendrix clucks his tongue.

"One drink, Reign. Come on, you got fans here," he tells me.

As I follow him back into his apartment, I'm surprised by the group that's gathered. Guys and girls, hanging around, smoking a bowl, drinking some beer and whiskey, it's a regular hangout. A gathering that reminds me of the early days in our Boston brownstone.

A pang of nostalgia cuts through my chest. I can still see

Levi pouring out tequila shots when we heard our first single on the radio.

"For you," a woman says, passing me a beer.

She's got bright red hair, deep green eyes, and big titties. They're barely concealed in a bikini top, the fabric triangles just covering her nipples.

"Thanks," I mutter, taking a swig.

Fuck, I miss Allegra. I move to the side of the room and call her. Maybe she'll want to meet me here to hang for a bit?

The call goes directly to her voicemail. I hang up.

Disappointment settles in my stomach even though it's irrational.

Maybe she's busy working. Or hanging with her friends.

Or, maybe, she's fucking avoiding me. Making the wall between us higher and thicker and re-enforced now that we kind of went on a date.

I drain my beer and gesture to a guy that I'll take a refill.

"I got that, honey," the redhead says.

I ignore her; I'm not in the mood for the antics of a fucking groupie.

I haven't been in a long-ass time.

TWENTY-ONE
ALLEGRA

THE KNOCK on my front door jars me awake.

It's not even a knock. Instead, it's an incessant tapping, punctuated by loud banging, followed by the sound of my name.

What the hell?

Bleary-eyed, I drag myself from bed. Slipping into a hoodie, I wrap my arms around my middle and slowly make my way to the door. I stop to peek out the peephole, releasing an exhale when I spot Derek.

"What the hell are you doing?" I ask, as I swing the front door open. Reaching out, I grab his arm and yank him forward. "You want to wake up the whole complex? What are you doing here?"

I waited all day for him to reach out. Other than his text this morning, he hasn't responded to my messages or calls. When I came home from work, I hoped he'd be here. But Derek ghosted me all day.

"Stellina," he slurs. His hands dart out to grip my waist and we sway together before I grasp the doorframe. "Fuck, baby."

My eyes widen. Derek's sauced. Is that why he was MIA all day? He left before I woke up this morning, sent me one text to say he's working, and got blitzed out of his mind?

"I love you, Allegra," he declares. The scent of beer and tequila wash over my face and I turn my head. "I fucking love you."

Then, his arms are around me, his face is buried in my neck, and I nearly buckle under his body weight.

He loves me. He fucking loves me. And this is how he tells me for the first time?

My heart cracks and my hurt soars.

"Derek," I say, giving him a little shake. "Derek, you're drunk."

"On you," he swears. "You make me fucking crazy."

"That's great to hear," I deadpan, walking him toward the living room couch. As shitty as I feel in this moment, I can't turn him away.

"Wait, did you drive here?" I ask seriously, worry churning my stomach.

"I'll always find you," he promises.

I sigh and give him a little push onto the couch. He drops instantly and curls on his side.

"You were right here, waiting for me," he carries on, twisting the proverbial knife.

I know I shouldn't take him literally. Not when he's drunk and spilling shit. But is that how he sees me? Reliable, dependable, waiting-on-him-and-his-bullshit Allegra?

Does he think I moped around all day, waiting for him to call me back? Wanting him to show up after my shift and take me to bed? Is that how he sees me? Worse, is that what I've done all day?

A moment later, the sound of Derek snoring whistles in the air.

I roll my eyes. Fisting my hands, I stare down at him. Half of me wants to punch him and demand why he showed up here. Why is he torturing me like this? The other half of me wants to shake some sense into myself.

Why do I keep falling for his shit? Why do I keep thinking he'll change?

This morning, I was ready to have a real conversation with Derek. I was willing to make myself vulnerable, to invite him in, to take a step forward.

And now? He leaves me hanging all day, doesn't reach out, save for a crappy text about work hours ago, and shows up drunk, spouting love declarations?

Turning on my heel, I leave him on the couch. I don't bring him a blanket. I don't prop his head up with a pillow. I leave him like a lump of coal and shut my bedroom door. Climbing back into bed, I lay still, seething as I stare at the ceiling.

Levi was right; I shouldn't trust Derek.

My friends warned me: keep it casual.

Disappointment swirls in my stomach. My chest aches.

Why do I keep repeating this pattern? Why do I keep thinking the outcome will be different? Why can't I move past Derek Reiner?

WHEN I WAKE in the morning, my head feels cloudy. My body is sore, and my neck is stiff. I heave out a yawn and swing my legs to the side of the bed. Derek's declaration from the night before greets me with the sunlight, and I groan, closing my eyes against both offenses.

I stand and make my way into the kitchen. I pause to glare at the lump on my couch, still snoring, still curled on his side.

God, even hungover and annoying, Derek looks hot. A slight stubble runs along his cheek. The slope of his nose, the angle of his cheekbone, the flutter of his eyelashes calls to me. I want to run my fingers over his face and memorize the details, imprint them through touch. His mouth is pursed, his lips full and gentle in sleep.

I'm used to seeing them pressed together in a harsh slant. Or curled up on one side in an amused smirk. Right now, he looks soft and peaceful. I fight the urge to run my fingers through his hair.

Instead, I recall how much he pisses me off. How hurtful his casual "I love you" landed when I was once desperate to hear those words from him. Last summer, he couldn't give them to me. Now, he says them drunk out of his mind and expects me to—what? Drop at his feet?

Why couldn't he tell me sober?

Is he capable of love on its own, without fleeing or getting drunk or a different destructive habit that undermines the thing he's trying to prove?

If Derek truly loved me, he wouldn't have stayed away all day yesterday only to resurface blitzed and begging. He would talk to me like the woman in his life. Not the afterthought, just waiting around for him to show up.

Shaking my head, I stomp to the kitchen. I'm loud as I bang cabinet doors closed, flip the faucet on, and grind coffee beans.

Now that I'm awake and annoyed, why should he get to sleep peacefully? Why should he nurse his hangover when I had my sleep interrupted by his obnoxious state and slurred words?

I pour myself a mug of coffee, add my favorite creamer, and take a big sip.

Placing it on the countertop, I heave out an exhale, and look at Derek.

His eyes are open and he's staring straight at me. When my gaze meets his, he winces.

"Good morning, sweetheart," I spit, a bite to my tone. "How'd you sleep?"

TWENTY-TWO
DEREK

SHE'S PISSED. Scratch that; she's fucking furious.

I force myself to sit up and groan at the pain in my head. My brain feels rattled, my throat cracked and dry, like sandpaper. Even my eyeballs ache, like I've got grains of sand caked underneath my eyelids.

Allegra's snide tone ricochets around my head.

I clear my throat.

"Oh, you need some water?" she asks, her voice infused with fake cheer. She's speaking too loudly.

I lift a hand to the side of my head and her chuckle causes my eyes to narrow.

She sighs and strides over to where I'm sitting, placing a glass of water on the coffee table.

"I hate myself for catering to you," she announces, more to herself than me.

"Thank you," I manage, lifting the glass to take a sip.

Allegra rolls her eyes, not bothering to respond.

The cool water wakes me up a little. My stomach feels queasy, the contents sloshing together, as I force myself to sit all the way up.

I watch Allegra for signs. Clearly, I showed up here drunk. Obviously, my waking up on the couch means I'm in the proverbial doghouse. But what the hell did I say—or worse, do—to warrant her reaction?

She regards me coolly, her arms crossed over her chest, her nails tapping against her arm. "You don't even know, do you?"

I clear my throat. "Know...which part?"

She sighs, staring up at the ceiling, begging some celestial being for patience. "You showed up drunk out of your mind."

I wince. "I know; I'm sorry."

"And told me you fucking love me," she spits out.

My neck snaps up and my eyes latch onto hers. The pain, mixed with longing, that I read in her irises pulls me up short. It knocks the breath from my lungs and causes my chest to ache. I hurt her, again.

"I do—" I start to explain myself. My actions. My fucking words that should make her feel good, not hurt.

"Don't say it," she cuts me off, her hand flailing forward. "I want to believe you, Derek. I want to fucking trust you. Instead, you left me hanging all afternoon—"

"I called you!" I throw out, defensive.

Surprise washes over her expression. "No, you didn't."

"Yeah. I called you from Hendrix's place. Part of me hoped you'd swing through. It went straight to voicemail."

Allegra's eyes close as some of her anger fades. "I didn't get. I passed by the NGO yesterday and sometimes have spotty service." She opens her eyes and sighs. "But still, I called you and messaged you several times.

"But you won't talk to me," I point out, zeroing in on the real issue. "I'm trying here, Allegra. And I know I'm messing some things up, but I'm giving you my best."

She chuckles and lifts an eyebrow. Her pointed look scans me.

I sigh. "Not right at this moment."

"I want something real, that I can count on," she says softly.

I grip the back of my neck. "You're not giving me a real shot."

"You haven't earned one yet," she reminds me.

I drop my head because, she's fucking right. And yet, how can I earn any semblance of trust if she's going to hold my past mistakes over my head? The shit from yesterday invades my mind, rolling back full force. Wanting to be honest with Allegra, as straightforward as possible, I confess the truth. "I woke up yesterday confused. Unsettled. You were sleeping so peacefully and all I wanted was a guitar. So I bounced, went to a studio my boy Hendrix owns, and played with this song—the song that's been messing with me—for hours."

"My song?" she murmurs, recalling that night from over the summer.

"Yeah," I admit, my voice low. "Can't get it right." My eyes hold hers for a long beat. She averts her gaze. I continue, "I texted you that I was getting some work done. I met up with Johan about the label, that turned into whiskey tasting and lunch. He tried to get me to play fucking golf." I scoff. "That'll be the day."

Allegra cracks an almost-smile. Yeah, picturing me on a golf course is laughable.

"Hendrix told me to roll back through. He had some local guys looking to jam, and to be straight with you, Allegra? I wanted to fucking play. Not to perfect a song or record or do the business side of shit. I wanted to *play*. With no expectations, with no end result in mind. So I went and it was…it was *good*."

She sits down next to me on the couch. She's curious because she's not pushing me through her apartment door. Still, her tone is sarcastic. "That why you drank?"

"No." I snort. "That came afterwards. Hendrix was having people over. I decided to grab a beer. And I missed you. So, I called you but when I got your voicemail, instead of bouncing, I had another drink and…"

"One thing led to another."

"Exactly," I say, relieved she understands.

"It always does with your kind."

"My kind?" I rear back.

She flicks her fingers at me. "Musicians. Artists. The creative ones who can't help but feel… I get it, Derek." She finally looks at me. "I get why you want to play; I know what music means to you. But for you to show up here, wasted, and tell me you love me after everything that happened between us… God, it felt like…"

"What?" I lean closer. Brush her hair behind her ear.

"It felt like a slap in the face. Like you were mocking me. Like I was the dumb, good, wifey kind of girl who sits at home and waits while her man is off, doing whatever the hell he wants, with whoever he wants."

"It's not like that, babe. I was in a shitty mood yesterday. I tried to see Levi but I'm not on his approved guest list. When I left the facility, I saw you called. I wanted to call you back but the headspace I was in, as pissed off as I was, I knew I'd just pick a fight with you. Plus, I'm still fielding fucking emails from my so-called dad… I went to the studio to blow off steam and make music. The drinks weren't part of my plan but once they happened, I just wanted you. I wanted to see you. Kiss you. Feel you and put you to bed." I grin at her.

She sighs heavily. I cup the side of her cheek and she leans into my touch. My thumb brushes across her bottom lip.

"I'm sorry, Allegra. I'm sorry for making you feel anything less than what you are. Which is everything." It's the most honest I can be, given the circumstances.

"I believe you, Derek. I know right now, you are sorry. You feel bad. You have regret or whatever. But I also know you're going to do it again. And again. And I'm not the kind of woman, nor do I want to be, who is going to sit around and take it. Wait for it. I want more. I want to be able to trust you. To let my guard down. To not overanalyze every detail wondering if it's a head game." She shakes her head. "Fuck, I deserve better."

Shit. That pulls me up short because I can't argue with it.

Even I know she deserves better than me. More.

I drop my hand from her face. "I know," I agree quietly.

She's not telling me anything new and yet, hearing her voice her wants helps me see them in a new way. If I don't get my act together, I'll lose her. Again.

And I'm not willing to do that.

"YOU LOOK ROUGH," Mav comments when I enter my condo.

I flip him the middle finger and he pretends to catch it and places it in his pocket. As if I'd blow him a fucking kiss. I roll my eyes.

"Let me guess..." Mav taps his finger against his bottom

lip, pretending to be thoughtful. But since no good thoughts arise from his brain, it's all a front. "You're hungover."

"Ding, ding, ding. Johnny, tell him what he's won," I deadpan.

Mav grins. "And you pissed off A."

I glare at him.

He drops his mouth open and brings his hands up to his cheeks, feigning shock. "I won more goodies?"

I snort. "Fuck off."

"What'd you do?"

"Told her I love her," I admit.

Mav rears back, surprise and disbelief mixing in his eyes. "Seriously? Did you get drunk beforehand and botch the delivery or afterwards when she told you to take a hike?"

"Why can't you buy your own place and not live at mine?" I ask.

He shrugs and eats a handful of Cheetos. "I'd feel bad about how lonely you'd be."

"You're not great company, Mav."

He laughs. "Before *and* afterwards, huh? Gonna be hard to come back from a double whammy."

"I shouldn't have shown up drunk."

"Never a good look," Mav agrees.

I wait for him to continue. He chomps on his fucking Cheetos and watches me.

"Are you going to say something useful?" I finally snap.

He grins. "Just waiting for you to ask, Reign."

"Fuck," I mutter.

"Say *please*," Mav carries on.

I glower at him. His grin widens.

"You need to woo her," he relents, tipping back his head. He lifts the bag over his mouth and shakes the last few Cheetos down his throat.

"You're disgusting."

"And a much better wooer," he says cheerily.

"What the hell is a wooer? How do you woo someone?"

"You have to do something nice for her, something that makes her feel special. Cared for."

"Like a date?"

Mav sighs and shakes his head. "You've set the bar so low, most girls would rather step over it. Be thankful you're a rockstar, Reign. You literally have nothing else going for you."

I flip him the middle finger again.

"Like a grand gesture," he clarifies.

I snap my fingers. "What if I take her bowling?"

Mav stares at me for a beat before erupting in laughter. "Oh, God. That's good. Yeah, yes, take her bowling."

"I can't tell if you're being serious," I growl. Turning away from Mav and his obnoxious laughter, I pour myself a cup of coffee. Resting my back against the countertop ledge, I take a sip and regard my friend. "I like bowling."

Mav sighs and drags a hand across his eyes. "Bowling could be cute. Honestly, it's not a grand gesture, but if you do something too nice, she may wonder if you've got ulterior motives. She's a smart girl and you're a shitty boyfriend, date, hell, even a shitty friend."

"Thanks for the ringing endorsement."

"If I haven't told you yet, I'm telling you now. I'll always pick Allegra's side over yours."

"You're living at my house."

He shrugs. "You won't kick me out."

"You know that—how?"

He shakes the empty bag of Cheetos. "I buy the good snacks. But I digress." He looks at me and shifts forward on his barstool. "Take her bowling. Take her out on a date. Do something easy and fun and normal. I think that's where you and A click the most."

"Doing normal things?" I wonder aloud.

"Yeah. She wants something she can trust. She wants emotional stability. You're searching for real, for someone who likes you for who you are instead of what you represent." He shrugs. "Normal activities, everyday things, meet both of your emotional needs. Bowling, beer, and pizza it is. Oh!" His eyes light up. "Maybe there will be an arcade too. You can win her an oversized teddy bear. She'd love that, having a souvenir of your time together. And it will make you feel tough and manly to carry around a giant purple panda."

"I don't like you as much as you think I do," I warn him.

He laughs and slips off the barstool. Moving back to the pantry, he rummages around for more snacks like a fucking raccoon.

I don't say anything else, but I think about Mav's assessment.

Allegra desires emotional stability and I'm searching for real.

Mav's right. Not that I'll give him the satisfaction of knowing it. But I do want real. I want to share something with a woman who sees me, who likes and respects and cares for me, because I'm Derek.

Not Reign. Not a Clover.

Just me.

And Allegra saw me for who I am from that first night, at her birthday bonfire.

I sealed my fate—and hers—the first time I kissed her.

TWENTY-THREE
ALLEGRA

"I HEARD YOU BLEW DEREK OFF," I say to my brother.

We're lounging outside, in the garden of his facility, drinking iced coffees.

"He come crying to you?" Levi scoffs.

"No." I shake my head. I hate that I'm about to stick up for Derek, but, "I think he was disappointed. I think he wants to make things right with you."

"Not gonna happen if he's screwing you over," Levi replies.

"What makes you think he's screwing me over?" I ask.

Levi's warned me away from Derek before, but other than bringing up Derek's behavior with women in the past, he's never had a real reason that pertains specifically to me.

Levi cuts me a look. It says, *Are you for real right now?*

I toss a hand in his direction, and he sighs.

"A, Derek's a rock god. Women drop their panties for him and offer to give him babies just for breathing."

I wince, not needing such a colorful visual.

"I fucking hate that he's been messing with your head, behind my back, too."

"It wasn't really behind your back," I clarify.

Levi narrows his eyes at me.

I shrug. "It's complicated. Things between Derek and me started a long time ago. And since then, there's always been this pull that's drawn me to him."

"That's what he wants you to think. You don't think he's had a magnetism with a hundred other women?" Levi asks.

His words land like a sucker punch, and for a moment, I'm too stunned to draw in a breath.

"I'm not trying to hurt you," Levi backpedals. "I just know how Reign thinks. It's with his dick. You're my sister, Allegra. I know I haven't shown up for you the way I should've, but I care about you. I fucking love you. And I hate that one of my best friends, my bandmate, would screw around with you, not talk to me about it, and continue doing it while I'm in fucking rehab."

I take another pull of my iced coffee. "When you say it like that..." I trail off, admitting that it sounds pretty shitty.

"Let me ask you something," Levi states. I glance at him. "If you truly were head over heels in love with Mckenna's brother—"

"She doesn't have one."

Levi snorts. "Fine. Nova's brother. Let's say you've got it bad for him, okay?"

"Yeah?" I ask.

"And it means something real."

"Okay."

"You wouldn't tell Nova? You wouldn't want her blessing or approval or anything?" Levi asks.

His words make sense, yet it isn't Derek's fault that we connected while Levi spiraled and then, checked into rehab. Still, I wouldn't keep the scenario Levi painted from Nova or any of my friends. Confusion swirls in my mind as frustration settles in my stomach. "I get your point."

"Good," Levi says.

"But the timing with Derek was during a difficult time for you. Everything between us was uncertain and everything with you was up in the air. Honestly? I think you should talk to him," I continue. "For the band."

"Why do you care so much about the band?"

"Seriously?" I give my brother a look. "Do you know me at all? Firstly, I know how much you care about the band. Plus, music is Derek's language, how he expresses himself. Thirdly, I adore Mav. I hate the thought that I'm somehow disrupting this group, this vibe, you've all had going on for years. It makes me feel guilty and... I already have enough shit on my plate to feel bad about."

Levi looks at me curiously. "You okay?"

"Yeah," I say. "Just working through stuff, you know? It would mean a lot to me if you talked to Derek. Just hear him out. I don't want to come between your friendship. Okay?"

"Fuck, fine," Levi agrees. I smile. "For you, A. And no promises on the outcome."

"That's fair."

"Besides, I'm getting out soon."

"You are?" I ask.

"Yeah," Levi laughs. "This isn't prison, you know. I can sign out at any time."

"How do you know when it's the right time?"

"I don't yet. I signed on for another sixty days and I'll follow through with that. Afterwards...well, I'll talk to my therapist and the support staff. But I'm aiming for that sixty-day mark."

I reach over and squeeze my brother's shoulder. "I'm proud of you, Levi."

He snorts. "Don't be; I'm nothing to be proud of."

"Yeah," I tell him, "you are. I'm glad you're back."

"Ahh, A..." He reaches over and wraps his arm around my neck, pulling me in for a side hug. "I missed you."

"Missed you more," I admit. I really did.

"HOW'S YOUR BROTHER DOING?" Dex asks as I tie on my apron.

I look up and smile. "Good. He's...he's like my brother again. Thanks for asking."

Dex nods. He crosses his arms over his chest and rocks back on his heels. "And the ex?"

I sigh. "Don't get me started on him."

Dex snorts. "Pissed you off or did you dirty?"

I tilt my head, thinking that over. "A little of both. I just, I don't know if he's capable of changing, you know? He says one thing but always ends up doing another."

Dex is silent for a moment. He slips behind the bar and fills up a glass of water, pushing it across to me. "You really think that? That people can't change?"

I chew the inside of my mouth. I want to believe that Derek can be better. Do better. But every time I start to trust that, he proves me wrong. He becomes unreachable. Or says something stupid. Or straight up leaves.

"I don't know," I say finally.

Dex gives me a smirk. "Huh. What about your brother?"

"Levi?"

"Yeah. You said he's like your brother again. Doesn't that mean he's changing? Growing? Improving?"

"I—I guess," I say, trying to answer Dex's question through a different lens. One that focuses on Levi instead of Derek. Levi has been honest and open; he's seeking support and working through the steps. Over the past few weeks, I have seen a profound change in him. He's not the same guy he was over the summer in Boston.

"What about me?" Dex asks.

I frown. "What about you?"

"I'm an addict, Allegra," he states. "I mean, I've been in recovery for nearly three years. But I battle those demons every damn day. I work real hard at it."

"You own a club," I blurt out.

Dex laughs again. "Exactly. I'm surrounded by temptation. And yet, every day I make the choice to stay clean. To not drink. To choose better and be more. A lot of my friends, people who knew me from before, would say I've changed. Are they right?"

"I think so," I say.

He narrows his eyes and looks at me for a long beat. "Do you?"

I roll my lips together and regard him curiously. What does he want me to say? What does he want me to admit?

"Changing, learning, and growing and evolving—it takes time. Takes a lot of work. Effort. Your ex, is he trying?"

I nod. I can't deny that Derek has been showing up for me, trying to talk to me, and being more present.

"Maybe the shit he pulls is unacceptable and unforgivable. That's for you, and only you, to decide. But I truly believe that people can change..."

"Why'd you do it? Get clean and commit to recovery?" I ask, wondering about his backstory. This guy, this larger-than-life man who has mentored me all semester, is an addict. And, until he told me, I had no idea.

Dex sighs. "A few years ago, a woman I dated a long time ago passed away."

My hand lifts to cover my mouth. "I'm sorry, Dex." Jesus, I wasn't expecting him to say that.

"Me too," he admits. "After she passed, I found out I had a son."

"You're a father?" I blurt out, shocked. I squint at him, as if it will help me see him more as someone's dad. For as long and as well as he's played a fatherly figure in my life, I never thought that he might have kids. That he might play this role for someone else.

"Apparently," he chuckles. "I never met my kid. But back then, I knew I couldn't. Not unless I was clean. Not unless I was the kind of dad a kid deserved to have. So, I got sober. I did the work. I turned my life around, bought Beirut." He holds his hand out to include the lounge. "And I've been trying to connect with my kid. At least now, if it works out, I can feel proud that I've accomplished something. That I'm doing something real and meaningful with my life. That when I wake up in the morning, I know my name and what I want to achieve during the day." He drops his elbows to the bar and leans forward. "People can change, A."

"Yeah," I say, seeing his point of view.

"Many would've said I was a hopeless case," he tacks on.

I grin and place my hand on his arm. "So, there's still hope for my ex?"

Dex laughs. "There's always hope."

Devy walks into the lounge and slips behind the bar. "What's good, Dex? Allegra?" she asks.

Dex fills her a glass of water like he did for me and

passes it to her. "All good, Devy. How's your grandma feeling?"

I smile, watching him interact with Devy. He worries about her, knows parts of her life, looks out for her, the same way he does for me.

Dex is a good boss but more than that, he's a good guy.

And he's living proof that people can change.

That there's still hope for Derek. For me and Derek.

Later that night, I receive a text that causes a new spark of hope to flicker.

Derek: I know you're working so I won't call until later... but will you go out with me, Allegra? On a date? A real one, where I pick you up and tell you how pretty you are and take you someplace silly and fun?

Me: Only if you bring flowers.

Derek: Tomorrow night, 7 p.m.?

Me: Yes.

I HOLD out a bouquet of wildflowers when she opens the door.

Her smile widens the moment she sees them. Reaching out, Allegra wraps a hand around the thick lace tying the stems together. "These are so beautiful, Derek."

"So are you," I say, unable to tear my eyes away from her beauty.

She rolls her eyes, but I note the pink that brightens the apples of her cheeks. Allegra steps back so I can slide past her and enter her place.

She moves to the kitchen and fills a vase with water before artfully arranging the flowers. "Wildflowers, huh?"

I glance at her. "They reminded me of you."

"Unable to be tamed?" she guesses.

I grin. "Bursting with color and beauty."

"Damn, Reign." She smirks, draping a hand over her chest. "You practice these lines before?"

I chuckle and close the space between us. "You never get basic lines, Stellina. You get my truths. Even more so now."

Surprise sparks in her irises, but she doesn't press for more of an explanation. Instead, she wipes her palms along her hips, drawing my attention to the simple denim miniskirt. "You ready?"

"Ready," I confirm.

As Allegra moves to the door, I can't help but check out her ass. She slips into a pair of Jordan dunks and slides on a lightweight leather jacket. She looks cool and laid-back. Put together but not trying too hard. I like that her confidence is still intact, her fire still burning bright.

I follow her into the dusk, and we slide into my Camry. Allegra relaxes in her seat, watching me as I drive to the bowling alley.

"Where are we going?" she asks.

"Bowling."

She snorts. "Wait, you're serious?"

I glance at her and grin. "As a heart attack."

A frown draws her eyebrows together.

"Have something...fancier in mind?" I guess.

"No," she says. "I, bowling is perfect." And then, softer, "It's something my family used to do. On the weekends. Levi..." She trails off.

Ah, shit. Did I mess this up? I reach over and place a hand on her thigh, my palm settling on the denim of her skirt, my flingers flirting over the bare skin of her leg. "We could go somewhere else," I offer.

"No." She shakes her head. "Really, bowling is perfect. Makes me...nostalgic, is all."

I squeeze her leg and she relaxes under my touch. I like that I can still soothe her. That after the way things went to shit between us, my presence still has a calming effect on her.

I pull into the bowling alley parking lot and park my car. "You ready? Because I'm pretty fucking good," I taunt.

Allegra laughs, the sound light and airy. "I'm a big deal on the lanes, Reiner."

I grin, loving her smack talk.

We enter the bowling alley and I direct us to the lane I reserved. It's already set with a bottle of wine chilling, a six pack of beer, and a bunch of appetizers and finger foods.

"Wow," she comments. "You actually planned this out."

I give her a playful wink. "I'm trying to impress this girl I'm crazy about."

"Shut up," she scoffs.

"I'm serious," I tell her. "I'm crazy about you. And tonight, this, it means something."

Allegra pauses, her eyes scanning mine. She must see the truth in them because her shoulders drop and a small grin plays at the corners of her mouth. "I'm going to grab shoes."

"I'm a size eleven," I call out.

She nods and returns a few moments later with shoes for both of us. While she was collecting bowling shoes, I set up our names on the screen.

When Allegra reads hers, she laughs. "Stellina?"

"My little star," I remind her.

"And Reign?" She gives me a look.

"Gonna rein your snark in," I mumble.

"Please," she huffs. "I'm gonna smoke your ass."

I snort. "Want to make a friendly wager?"

Allegra's eyes sparkle, sage green expanding into pools of chocolate. "How friendly?" She bites her bottom lip and I nearly groan.

I expected more shit talking, not her enthusiastic partic-ipation in making things dirtier than they need to be.

I smack my lips together. "If I win, we spend the night together. It doesn't have to be sexual; we can stay up talking and watching movies. Like old times. But we spend time hanging out together."

Her gaze softens and she nods. "Okay."

"Okay. And if you win?" I raise an eyebrow.

"If I win," she sighs. "If I win, you come visit Levi with me. I'll get you on his list. And you talk to him, for real. Try to heal this rift between you. For the sake of the band and for me."

That pulls me up short. I freeze and look at her curiously. "That's what you want? It means that much to you?" Is it because she knows this thing between us is for real? Or is it because Levi's giving her a hard time and she wants to appease him?

"Yes," she says simply.

"Okay," I agree. Hell, I'll do nearly anything she asks of me if it means another shot with her. "You're up first."

Allegra grins wickedly and picks up her bowling ball. I sit back in my seat, ready to toss out some words of encouragement. But my girl executes perfect fucking form as she lets the bowling ball go down the alley, just right of center, and knocks a damn strike.

"Shit, Allegra!" I call out, clapping.

She spins toward me and does a little shimmy. "Told you I'd smoke ya!"

I snort, wrapping an arm around her waist and pulling her against my chest. "You were serious about this being a family pastime."

Her eyes dart to mine, serious and solemn. She lifts her chin in a silent challenge. "I don't lie, Derek."

That cuts because I'm a big fucking liar and we both know it. But, "I know. It's something I admire about you."

She sighs, her expression easing. "I'm not going to go easy on you."

I grip her tighter. "I expect nothing less from you."

She smiles, I grin, and we play three games.

Allegra wins them all.

"A clean sweep!" she announces after the final game concludes.

I groan. "I thought I'd win at least once."

"Presumptuous."

"Come here," I say, tugging her toward the back of the bowling alley. "Let's have a go at darts."

At that, my girl freezes.

I glance over my shoulder and grin. "Not so fucking confident now, are ya?"

Allegra smirks. She wrinkles her nose and it's so adorable I tap my finger against it. "I'm not good at darts," she admits.

"Let me teach you," I offer, my voice low.

Between our bowling, we polished off the bottle of wine and I had two beers. We're not drunk, but we are veering toward tipsy. That type of buzz when everything feels great. Lighter than normal, brighter than it should be, and happy on a scale that borderlines giddy. I've already made arrangements for a driver to meet us here and take us home in my car.

My hand slides from her waist to the soft swell of her ass. I pinch lightly and Allegra squeaks.

"Fine," she agrees.

Grinning, I take her hand and guide her to the dart board.

I grab the darts and demonstrate a round before pulling them out again and passing them to her. "Here," I say, placing a hand on her hip. "Widen your stance. Put your right foot forward." I tap my foot against hers and position her. "You wanna use these three fingers." I show her how to properly hold a dart. Wrapping her fingers around the dart, I relax her grip. "Then, aim and throw. Just have fun, Stellina."

She nods and closes one eye as she focuses on her aim.

I don't bother telling her she can keep it open. It's fucking cute as hell to watch her squint and take aim. She lets the dart sail and when it snags on the board, albeit not in the scoring range, she tosses her arms in the air.

"I did it!" she exclaims.

I laugh. "You did. Try again." I hand her the second dart. I give her a few more instructions and watch as my girl gets better which each throw.

I win but after witnessing her happiness playing darts, don't bother rubbing it in her face.

Instead, I wrap her in a hug, kiss her cheek, and murmur, "You did real good, love."

She looks up at me, her eyes open. There's a vulnerability, a layer of trust, I haven't witnessed since the summer. The mask she's been sporting slips and she looks like the girl I first fell in love with again. The girl who wears her heart on her sleeve.

"I know I won at bowling," she says.

I snort. "Yeah, me too."

"But will you still spend the night with me, Derek? Can we still hang out and watch movies?" Her voice is soft, her eyes wide. Beautiful and beguiling.

I nod. "It would be my honor, Stellina." Then, I brush my lips over hers. Softly. Gently. "Want to go to the arcade?" I whisper against her mouth.

She smiles and shakes her head. "I'd rather you light me up instead of a game board."

I snort and dip my chin. My eyes find hers and hold. "I'd prefer that too," I admit, right before I kiss her again.

This time, I wrap my arms around her waist. Her fingers cling to the material at the back of my shirt. Our mouths collide, our tongues dance, and we kiss passionately. Like it's been too damn long since we've tasted each other.

Because it has been.

I CAN'T KEEP my hands off him and I don't want to. I think he feels the same way because as soon as we make it to my front door, his hands on are me. His fingers in my hair, his mouth on my neck, his touch everywhere all at once. Getting the door unlocked is a challenge, with both of us wanting to lose ourselves in each other.

"Your door," Derek reminds me as I press a kiss to his collarbone.

"Uh-huh," I agree, but his hands are squeezing my waist and I'm arching into his chest. I drag in a ragged inhale and my breasts scrape across his hard abdomen.

"Here," he murmurs, his voice low and needy. He takes my keys and unlocks the front door.

The second we're inside, he flips the lock.

I'm already popping the button on my skirt. It slides to the floor, and I step out of it. I'm desperate for Derek. For his kiss and his touch and his skill. He was the first man to ever make me come, and right now, after a few glasses of wine and a fantastic date, I want all the orgasms.

I kick my skirt to the side and move to lift the hem of my shirt.

"Wait." Derek's voice is guttural.

I freeze, a wave of panic locking down my limbs. Is he going to turn me down? Does he not want me? Or this?

My cheeks heat and my eyes dart to his.

Derek steps closer and touches my waist. His eyes are dark and unreadable. "Stellina..." He sounds half stran-gled. With want? With worry? "This is real for me, beauti-ful. This isn't a night or a moment, this is everything. And fuck, I know I said that and bailed. But before this goes further, I need you to know that I'm all in. I want you, baby. I want every fucking thing with you. No one has ever made me feel the way you do. So please, don't give yourself to me unless this is real for you. I have no fucking right to ask, but I am. I want all of you, Allegra. Every fucking part."

I drop my arms to my sides and stare up at him. Is he serious? Could this be for real?

"Say something," he whispers.

"I want this to be real," I murmur.

He brushes his fingers along my cheek, tucks my hair behind my ear. "It is. It's always been real."

I nod and lift my chin. "I want you too, Derek. All of you."

"That's all I need to know." Then, his mouth is on mine. This time, his hands work my shirt up, over my head, and discard it on the floor.

His hands are in my hair. Mine are tugging at his cloth-ing. He sheds his shirt and jeans quickly. Then, I'm back in his arms, his knee pressing between my thighs, his hands on my ass.

His frame folds over mine, not breaking our kiss, as our

hands hungrily track each other's bodies. Remembering. Memorizing. Caressing.

"Come here," Derek bites out. He swings me up into his arms and carries me, like a prized possession, into my bedroom. He places me down in the center of my bed and crawls over me, his body coiled tightly, his eyes blazing. "Fuck, love. I missed you so goddamn much."

My knees fall open for him and he settles between my legs. His hand cups around my cheek, his fingers anchoring to the back of my head, as he lifts my face to his and kisses me earnestly. Derek's tongue slips inside my mouth, my eyes flutter closed, and my arms wind around his neck.

My breasts press into his chest, and he shifts to he can slide one hand down to fondle my right breast. His touch is firm and sure. A moment later, he slides lower, and his mouth replaces his fingers as he deftly removes my bra. Then, my nipple is in his mouth and his tongue laves against the pebbled bud.

Heat rushes between my legs and I tilt my pelvis up, wanting him to provide the friction I crave.

"Patience, beautiful," he warns. "We have all night." He plays with my left breast.

My fingers run through his hair. His head comes up and he smiles salaciously before slipping even lower. He brings my right thigh up and hooks it over his shoulder as he plants his face in between my thighs and drags a finger over the center seam of my panties.

I shudder from the sensation.

"How wet are you, love?" Derek murmurs, repeating his ministration.

"Wet," I murmur.

"Hmm?" he questions. He pushes the satiny material to the side and blows lightly on my aching pussy.

I shudder again and Derek grins. His eyes are hooded and filled with lust as he looks at me. Slowly, he lowers his mouth and drags his tongue up my slit.

"Derek," I pant.

"Yeah, baby?" He licks me again, long and slow. "Fuck, you're soaked," he decides. Two of his fingers play with my pussy as he kisses lightly along my inner thighs, nips at my clit, and turns my ache into a persistent throb.

I can't think as I stare at him, so turned on, my fingers tremble. I move to palm my breast and Derek's eyes heat.

"Show me," he encourages.

I bring my hands to my breasts and arch into them, my fingers pinching at my nipples. Derek leans back to take in my show, his hungry gaze burning. Then, he takes my right hand and moves it in between my legs. "Show me how you touch yourself, Stellina."

"Fuck," I swear, staring at him. Is he serious? He wants me to—

"Don't be shy, baby," he says, cupping his length through his boxer briefs. He's hard for me and witnessing that gives me the confidence I need to drag two fingers through my arousal.

My eyes nearly roll back in my head.

I gather my want and bring it up to my clit. Rubbing gentle circles around the tiny bud of nerves, I moan.

"Eyes here," Derek demands.

I look at him. My mouth waters when I note he pulled out his cock and is now stroking it in bold, daring passes.

"Fuck, you're something else," he tells me. Positioning himself at my pussy, he drags his hard cock through my soaked folds.

"Derek," I pant. God, that feels good. Better than good.

Heavenly. I love seeing my arousal glisten on his cock. I shimmy up, wanting him to enter me.

He laughs, the sound husky. "Not yet, Stellina." He shifts again and his mouth is between my thighs. His tongue replaces my fingers. He licks and sucks at my most sensitive parts like he's feasting. His hands plant on my inner thighs and hold me open as he eats me up like he'll never get enough.

His intensity, coupled with my wanton groans, have me cresting in seconds. "Derek, oh God, baby," I manage before I break apart. My body pulses as streams of white-hot pleasure shoot through my limbs. I come hard and long, a tireless wave of bliss I want to ride forever.

Before my ripples of pleasure subside, Derek enters me on a sharp thrust. On a roar of satisfaction.

"Fucking hell, Stellina," he swears as he begins to move.

"Oh God." I arch under him. I love how he stretches me, fills me, makes all the emptiness disappear. "Derek," I pant, a warning flashing through my mind. "I'm not on birth control."

He moves to pull out.

"No." I shake my head. "Keep going." I lift my hips.

His tortured eyes meet mine. The hunger in them is insatiable but so is the concern. The *love*.

"I'll pull out," he promises.

I nod, not caring about anything beyond this moment.

Derek slows his pace, rocking into me on slow, controlled thrusts. His mouth finds mine and he kisses me deeply. It's passionate. As his cock slides in and out, it's the steady rhythm that brings me back to the peak. Our connection isn't wild and heady.

It's meaningful and sensual. Derek's touches are caresses. His kisses are promises. My touches are endearments. We make love and it's nothing like I've ever known before.

Swells of emotion gather behind my eyes. My limbs feel weightless, my body full, my mind blank as Derek and I come together. It's beautiful and effortless and everything.

"Please," I plead.

"I got you, love," he promises. "I'm right here."

I press my face into the crook of his neck. Derek gathers me to his chest. His arms band around me and his body covers mine like shelter. His kisses sustain me like sustenance. His presence envelops me, and again, I break apart. But it's more than that. In his hold, I find myself again.

I find him and home and us.

"Derek," I pant.

"Fuck, beautiful," he swears. "I'm gonna come for you, baby."

"Come for me," I beg.

He does. On a guttural, raw groan, Derek's body tightens, the veins on his forearms pop, he throws back his head, and quickly pulls out. Hot spurts of his desire stream across my lower abdomen.

Then, he collapses on top of me. Rolling to the side, he brings me with him. He holds me close, his cum smearing, sticky between our skin.

But I don't care. Nothing matters except this moment.

Our noses brush and Derek stares at me. Looking deeply into my eyes, he says, "I love you, Allegra. I love you so fucking much it terrifies me."

"Shh," I soothe him, placing a hand on his cheek. His stubble presses into my palm. "I love you too, Derek. I always have."

"Stellina." His eyes flash, something akin to pain and regret and blinding love, before his lips brush over mine.

"So much for the movie," I murmur against his lips.

He chuckles. "Or talking?"

"We'll be talking," I promise.

"Good." He kisses me again.

We stay like that, wrapped in each other's arms, kissing and whispering and caressing, until my eyes close and sleep drags me under.

At some point, Derek slips from the bed. A moment of panic seizes me, but before I can react, he's back. I feel the warm washcloth move between my legs and wipe over my thighs, up my stomach. Then, he's beside me again. His arms wrap around me and hold me against his chest.

In Derek's arms, I drift into a deep sleep.

THE SCENT of coffee rouses me in the morning.

I open my eyes and grin when I see him. He's placing a mug of coffee down on my nightstand.

"Good morning," I say. I yawn and wipe sleep from my eyes as I sit up.

"Morning, Stellina." Derek brushes a quick kiss over my lips. "How'd you sleep?"

"Like the dead," I admit.

"Yeah," he agrees. "Your snores were a giveaway."

I wrinkle my nose. "I don't snore."

He chuckles. "You're cute when you lie to yourself."

I roll my eyes.

Derek sits beside me and plants one hand next to my hip, leaning into my space.

His eyes bore into mine, studying me.

"What?" I ask, a little self-conscious.

"Last night."

"What about it?" My nerves flare to life.

"It was the realest moment of my life," he admits. "I meant every damn thing I said, Allegra. I want this with you. This is for real. You're fucking it for me."

"You said that last night," I remind him.

"It's worth mentioning this morning," he replies, the corner of his mouth curling up. "I don't want any confusion between us. So, I'm telling you again: I love you. I mean it. It's not the sex or the alcohol or anything else. It's you. I'm in love with *you*."

I melt at his words. Grinning, I bite my bottom lip. "Good. I love you too."

"I know."

I roll my eyes and snort, smacking him in the chest.

"Hey!" He grabs my wrist.

"You don't have to be so cocky about it."

Derek chuckles. "Old habits die hard."

"Whatever."

"You hungry?" he asks.

"Why?" I ask playfully, tilting my head. "You want to take me on a breakfast date?"

"I want to take you on all the dates," he confirms. "We're dating now, Allegra. Wait..." He shakes his head. "Scratch that. We're more than dating, baby. You're my girlfriend."

I rear back slightly. While I get that Derek's being sincere, I didn't expect him to slap a label on it. "You don't strike me as someone who's into labels."

"I'm not. But deep down, you are."

I blush because he's right. For as much as I pretend otherwise, I like knowing where we stand. "I want to be your girlfriend."

"Good. Because I am most definitely your fucking man," he says before his mouth lands on mine.

Derek kisses me hard. Then, he proves his worth as my new beau and makes me come twice before depositing me in the shower. When I'm dressed and ready, he takes me to brunch.

We enter the restaurant holding hands and Derek doesn't bat an eye at the cell phones that turn in our direction. He doesn't care about the flashes that capture our photos, or the posts that pop up on social media.

He doesn't have eyes for anyone but me.

I NEVER THOUGHT I'd enjoy folding laundry. Or watching reruns of throwback sitcoms. Or hanging by my phone, waiting for a girl to call.

But Allegra isn't any girl. She's mine. And I love every second I spend with her.

As we settle into a real relationship, the doubts and concerns I've harbored for years melt away. I'm not tempted by other women. I don't even see them. I'm not worried about balancing the band and my relationship. Allegra respects and encourages my time at the studio.

Save for Levi, even the opinions of our friends are an endorsement.

Mav hugged Allegra and slapped me on the back. "About damn time," he quipped when we told him the news.

Allegra's friends also welcomed me with open arms, although Mckenna squinted at me and demanded I treat her friend right. I promised I would.

After that, we partied together like we've been friends, a

group of friends, for years. It's normal and nostalgic. Exciting and effortless.

Mav teases Mckenna relentlessly. She ignores him completely.

Nova brings along the football player she's seeing and he's a cool, down-to-Earth guy.

Ivy makes outrageous demands that include bringing her on a future tour.

And Allegra? My girl smiles and laughs and spreads her sunshine. She melts into me when I hold her. She kisses me back with as much heart and heat as I pour down her throat.

She dies her hair back to its natural brown shade.

"You look gorgeous," I tell her when she walks into my condo after her appointment at the hair salon.

She twirls her finger around the blunt ends. "It's still a bit short but... I'm going to grow it back out."

"I like it," I say, meaning it. I like everything Allegra does. "Mav just went out to grab dinner. You hungry?"

She shrugs and slips onto a barstool. "I can eat."

I nod and send off a quick text to Mav to grab some of Allegra's favorites from the Tex-Mex restaurant we frequent.

"I've been thinking," I say, sliding onto the stool beside her.

"Uh-oh." Her voice is teasing but I note the flicker of uncertainty in her gaze.

Damn. We're definitely making progress and Allegra has no problem being sweet and affectionate toward me, but a part of her still worries the other shoe is going to drop. And that's on me.

I filled her with so much fucking doubt, it clouded the way she views herself. It muddled her ability to trust her own judgement. And I hate that for her.

"We should go see Levi," I state.

Her eyes clear and she lets out a little laugh. "Oh, right. This is because I won bowling, isn't it?"

I snicker. Wrapping my fingers around the underside of her barstool, I pull her closer until I can cage her knees in between mine. "This is because I love you and it's important to you."

Allegra beams. With gratitude shining in her eyes and her gorgeous hair back to its dark color, she looks like the girl I fell for in Boston. Leaning over, I press a quick kiss to her cheek. "Set up the date and time. I'll be there."

"Okay, well..." She pauses. "I was going to visit Levi Thursday afternoon. I have a late shift Wednesday night, but we could drive up early on Thursday?"

"Or I could pick you up Wednesday night and drive us up after your shift. We could stay at a hotel and do brunch the next morning and then visit Levi..." I trail off, gauging her reaction.

Her eyebrows tug inward. "Seriously? You want to just—"

"Have hot hotel sex with you?" I cut her off. "Yeah, I do."

Allegra laughs. It's the best music I've ever heard. "Okay. Sure. Let's do that. I'll see if I can leave early. If it's not busy I may be able to head out at midnight."

"That would be perfect," I agree. Mentally, I'm sorting through my favorite hotels. The ones with the best beach views, brunches, swimming pools, and swim-up bars.

"Cool. Okay! I'm excited." She's so damn cute.

I grin. "Me too, baby."

The front door swings open and Mav enters. "I got extra chips and guac, A!"

"Mav!" She springs from her barstool to help Mav carry in the takeout bags.

"How you doing, girl?" he asks, kissing the crown of her head.

"All good. Derek's whisking me away this week," she answers.

"Is he?" Mav gasps, feigning surprise as his eyes cut to mine. "Where are you taking our fair maiden?"

I snort. "We're going to visit Levi on Thursday afternoon. Might as well have a decent brunch beforehand. Maybe a swim."

Mav pauses and his eyes study mine for a long moment. "Good," he says finally. "That's good. You and Levi should talk. You need to clear the air before he finishes rehab."

"When's that?" I ask, completely out of the loop with my best friend, save what Allegra or Maverick divulge.

"Another two or three weeks," Allegra responds quietly.

"Time's ticking, Reign." Mav's voice holds more of a warning. *Fix this shit with Levi and move past it so the rest of us can.*

I lift my chin at Mav to let him know I caught his message.

He places a brown paper bag down in the center of the island. "Let's eat."

Allegra and I pull out the takeout containers and the three of us sit around the island, eating and talking, until Mav calls it a night.

Then, I lead my girlfriend into my bedroom and undress her slowly. I spend time moving my hands and mouth over every inch of her sweet skin. I don't take a second of our time together for granted. Instead, I worship her, care for her, and love her the best way I know how.

When I finally find my release, her name is on my lips, her smile imprinted on my soul.

Allegra is my everything and there isn't a damn thing I wouldn't do for her.

"HAVE A SAFE TRIP," Mav tells me as I swipe my car keys off the countertop.

"Thanks, mate. What are your plans?" I ask.

"Just hanging. May meet up with A's friends for drinks. Ivy invited me out," he says.

"Ivy's a sweet girl," I toss out, trying to get a read on Mav. Is he into one of Allegra's friends?

"Yeah. She's chill," he agrees noncommittally. Then, "I think I drive Mckenna fucking nuts." He grins. "She's a riot."

Ah, he's always had a thing for redheads and with her strawberry-blonde waves and skeptical navy eyes, Mckenna Byrne could give Mav a run for his money. I grin but don't give my two cents. "Have fun."

"Will do. See you later." Mav lifts a hand in farewell.

I grab the backpack I packed with my overnight necessities and clean clothes for tomorrow and head to my car. I made reservations at a trendy boutique hotel situated right on the ocean. It offers a delicious brunch menu and a gorgeous view of the water. It's fun, edgy, and private—all things I know Allegra will appreciate.

I turn my car toward Beirut, my hands tapping out a rhythm on the steering wheel. When Allegra messaged me an hour ago that her boss was letting her slip out early, my excitement jumped.

I can't wait to spend time with my girl, away from our daily grind, and get lost for a little while. When her semester is over, I'm going to whisk her away for real. Maybe Paris. She's always wanted to go there. Or Costa Rica. Mav has great things to say about his favorite destination.

I pull into the parking lot of the lounge and park around back. Allegra said to slip in through the back entrance and meet her by the staff lockers.

I turn off my car and approach the back door. Even though it's nearing midnight, the area is well lit, and the door is propped open.

I knock twice just to announce my arrival. "Hello?" I call out as I enter the hallway.

"Have a good time, Allegra. Drive safe," a male voice is saying.

"Thanks, Dex. And thanks for letting me take off early," Allegra's voice rings out.

I follow her voice. The hallway widens and I spot her standing in the doorframe to what I assume is her boss's office.

"Hey," I say.

She spins when she sees me. "You're here!" She steps into my embrace and presses up on her tippy-toes to kiss my cheek. "Come here. You've gotta meet Dex."

Allegra takes my hand and pulls me through the doorframe. The man behind the desk stands. He's tall and formidable looking. Allegra's spoken of him several times, but I never expected him to be so young. In his forties. Or good-looking, with stylish dark hair and deep brown eyes.

"Hey," I say, holding out a hand. "I'm Derek."

The man stands still, his eyes studying me with an intensity that puts me on edge. But he's not giving off creepy vibes. Instead, his expression is almost emotional, with hope flaring in the depths of his gaze.

"Uh, Dex? This is my boyfriend, Derek…" Allegra trails off as Dex clears his throat.

He takes my hand, shaking it. His grip is firm, his shake solid. He clears his throat again and something flashes through his eyes. "Good to meet you, Derek." His voice cracks on my name. Another clearing of his throat. "I'm Derek too. Derek Madden. But everyone calls me Dex."

I freeze.

Derek Madden.

My so-called father.

The man who has sent me letters via his lawyer for over a fucking year.

Here, in LA, as Allegra's boss. Or mentor. Or fucking father figure.

I glare at him, hating that we have the same whiskey-colored eyes. How the hell did he track me down? Did he know that Allegra is my girl?

Of course, he fucking knew.

I let out a harsh chuckle.

How could he not?

Is that why he hired her? Is that why she brought me here?

My gaze turns to Allegra. Did she fucking set me up? Is this one of her interventions? As if clearing the air with Levi isn't enough?

But Allegra's mouth is wide open and she's gawking at Dex like he just steamrolled her.

I shake my head. Drop my hold on Allegra's hand. The room tilts before me. Floaters appear in my peripheral vision. My hands curl into fists, my throat tightens. My heart beats erratically, a too-high, too-fast thrumming sound that pulses in my eardrums.

"Derek, I've been wanting to speak with you for years," Dex continues. Or is it Derek too? "I'm so happy to finally meet—"

"No," I cut him off. He doesn't get to just say his piece, flip me his shit, now. Not when I'm supposed to spend one-on-one time with my girl. Not when I was just getting my shit sorted.

For the first time in fucking months, my head isn't a goddamn mess. Allegra and I are good. Forging forward. Together.

And now...this guy tosses me this curveball and just expects me to catch it? And what? Do what?

"Fuck this," I murmur.

"Derek!" Allegra gasps.

I swing toward her, my eyes narrowed. "Did you know?" I spit out even though I know the answer.

She sucks in an inhale, a hand rising to her chest like I hurt her. Well, no surprise there, huh? It's not the first time I let Allegra down.

Who was I kidding, thinking I could do this? Be a normal, emotionally available, present boyfriend? My life is too twisted, my head too messed up. My past has finally caught up with me and it's with a man Allegra, my fucking Stellina, admires.

A man I have no desire to get to know.

Not when he abandoned me. Left me in the goddamn system with abusers like Simon.

"Fuck," I swear again. Then, I turn around and barrel out of the office.

"Derek! Wait!" Allegra calls after me.

I press both palms against the door, so it swings wide open.

"Let him go, A," Dex's low voice cuts the air. A thread of concern weaves through his words, as if I'm somehow dangerous. As if he doesn't want Allegra with me.

The thought makes me snort derisively.

Does he think I'd hurt my girl? Does he think she can't trust me? Does he see himself as her fucking father figure when he doesn't know the first damn thing about showing up as a parent?

Overwhelmed and confused, I slip behind the steering wheel of my car.

My gaze cuts to the bar once and my heart fucking breaks when I see Allegra. She's standing right outside the door, her big brown eyes wide with worry. Her fingers twist together in front of her, as if she doesn't know what to do with her hands.

She stares at me like her heart is breaking. For me. For her.

For my never-present father.

I shake my head once and flip the ignition on my car. Then, I drive away from Beirut.

I don't look in my rearview mirror.

I learned a long time ago to never look back.

Besides, I don't want to witness the heartache on Allegra's face.

Not when I already carry it around with me, like a constant reminder.

A self-fulfilling prophecy.

"DEREK!" I scream as his taillights disappear down the street.

"Let him cool off," Dex advises, his hand steady on my shoulder.

I spin toward him, my eyes wild. "You're Derek Madden?" I sound accusatory.

He nods. "I am. But everyone—"

"Calls you Dex," I bite out, finishing his sentence. "Did you know?" I demand, my arm flailing to the side to indicate the place where Derek's car was parked. "Is that why you—"

"No," he cuts me off forcefully. "I'm—Jesus, Allegra, I'm just as surprised as you. Come into my office; let's talk."

I regard him coolly but, wanting answers, follow Dex inside. On the short walk to his office, I call Derek. He ignores the call.

Me: Derek... Please, come back. Please.

I glare at the blank screen, but he doesn't call me back. Or respond to my text.

Dex sighs heavily. "Take a seat, A."

I plop into the chair in front of his desk. It's a seat I've occupied countless times since the night Dex found me drunk in the back alley. But this time, it feels strained. Almost like I'm betraying Derek by being here, hearing Dex out before my boyfriend.

"I swear I didn't know that Derek Reiner is your ex," Dex starts. He folds his hands together on top of his desk. He looks tired. Older. As if meeting Derek and having him take off aged him.

"I remember Derek mentioning you last summer," I murmur.

Dex nods. "I've been trying to connect with him for over a year. Ever since—"

"You learned you had a son," I whisper, my eyes widening as I remember Dex's story.

"Since I got sober and got my life on track," he amends.

"He's the son you regret not having a relationship with. The one you didn't know existed until his mother passed."

"Exactly," Dex breathes out. "Fuck, he was right here. This whole time. I thought he went back to Boston after his whiskey label but..."

"He stayed."

Dex nods. "He stayed for you." Even though it should be a question, he voices it as a statement.

I shrug. "Things were going good between us. Finally, we were in sync and planning a future together."

Dex frowns. "Why do you think anything's changed?"

I snort. "You don't know Derek." His face falls and I regret my word choice. Still, I forge on. "This is going to crush him. If only he would sit and talk to you."

"You don't think he will?"

I shake my head. "I don't know. I should get home. I

need to see him. Talk to him. I'll tell him what you told me, Dex. I'll tell him you didn't know."

"I'd appreciate that," Dex agrees. "I've tried to do right by him, Allegra. I tried to go through all the proper channels. To ensure I wasn't crossing any lines. I just, I want to know my boy. And if I had known he was your boyfriend, I still would've done it by the book. I want a real relationship with him, that's it. I want whatever he's willing to give me."

"I understand," I say. I hate how defeated Dex looks. "You're a good man, Dex."

He chuckles humorlessly and it reminds me of Derek. "I should've been better."

I roll my lips together to avoid telling him how similar he and his son are. It's not the right time. Right now, I need to find my boyfriend.

"I'll see you later this week," I say, standing from the chair.

"Let me give you a ride home," Dex offers.

Since Derek dropped me off for my shift, I mutter a thanks and follow Dex to his car. For the entire ride, I call and text Derek. He never picks up or replies to my messages. I send two texts to Mav, but both go unanswered.

I debate going to his condo but don't want to put Dex or Derek in another awkward situation. Instead, I thank Dex for the ride and enter my apartment.

Then, I sit on the couch, and leave Derek a voicemail.

"Hey, Derek, it's me. I know that you're angry and confused. You probably feel blindsided. But I need you to know that I had no idea Dex is Derek Madden. And he had no idea that you are my boyfriend. This is seriously one of those crazy, small world, six degrees of separation things. Please, call me. Or come over. I want to see you and talk to you. I want to know you're okay. I want to explain things I know and have Dex explain the rest. You deserve to know the full story, Derek. Come home to me. I love you."

I end the call and spend the next thirty minutes pacing my apartment.

When my phone rings, I snatch it up, my stomach sinking when I spot Mav's name on the screen.

"Are you with him?" I answer.

"Allegra!" Mav hollers through a swell of voices. "Hang on." The sound of voices quiets. "Hey, I'm out with your girls."

"Oh yeah," I mutter, closing my eyes. "Kenny mentioned that."

"Oh?" Mav says. "What else did Mckenna say?"

"Did you get my messages?" I ask. Now is not the time to joke around with Mav or tell him that he drives Mckenna bananas with his playful teasing.

"Yeah. Reign's not with me. What's going on? I thought you guys would be on your way up the coast by now."

I sigh. "It's a long story but...Derek took off. I'm trying to find him. I'm worried about him, Mav."

"Fuck," Mav swears, hearing the seriousness in my tone. "All right, let me bounce. I'll meet you at Derek's?"

"Do you care if I stay here? I'm hoping he comes over," I say.

"Okay. I'll call you as soon as I'm at his place," Mav promises.

"Thanks, Mav."

He disconnects the call. My pacing continues.

Is Derek at a bar getting shitfaced? Is he driving around aimlessly, his mind turning over parts of his past? Is he alone or with people? Is he angry or sad?

"Why the hell won't you talk to me?" I growl, muttering to my empty apartment.

I know Dex blindsided Derek, but this is an opportunity for him. For both to get to know each other. And I know they would like each other if Derek gave Dex a chance.

"Why are you so damn stubborn?" I toss out.

My heart hammers and my thoughts twirl. Every minute that passes without a response from Derek feels like an eternity. My concern spikes. My thoughts swirl faster, half panicked and all assuming awful scenarios.

By the time Mav calls, I'm out of my mind with worry.

"Maverick," I answer.

"Allegra." Mav pauses and takes a deep inhale. "Fuck, girl, he's gone."

"Gone?" I murmur, my eyebrows pulling together. I sit down on the edge of the couch. "What do you mean? Do you think he went to the hotel? Or maybe he needs to clear his head? Have you talked to your brother? Or—"

"He cleared out his stuff," Mav cuts me off, putting an end to my delirious stream of consciousness. "Grabbed his passport. He's gone, A. And I don't know if he's coming back."

The phone slips from my hand as my chest physically aches. I feel my heart crack and a tear slip down my cheek. In the distance, I hear Maverick calling my name but I'm unable to form words.

I'm unable to do anything but wonder what the hell just happened?

A wave of déjà vu washes over me.

Worried and all alone, I let it drag me under.

I beg it to drown me.

Allegra

"I'M PROUD OF YOU," I tell my brother when he slides into the passenger seat of my car after stowing his suitcase in the trunk.

"Good to see you, A." Levi grins, reaching over the center console to pull me into a hug.

I breathe in the scent of his cologne and let him hold me for an extra moment. It feels nice, safe, and steady to be in my brother's embrace.

"You ready to go home?" I ask.

Levi snorts. "I can get my own place."

"It'll be fun to be roommates again," I reply.

"Yeah," he agrees. "I really appreciate the offer to stay with you, A. Even though I feel better, my head's clearer than it's been in years, I'm...well, I'm fucking scared to be left to my own devices."

I flash him a smirk as I direct my car toward the exit. We've got a drive before us, but it's perfect as Levi and I have a lot to catch up on. "Mav's nearby too," I remind him.

"Yeah," he says. "But he's heading to Costa Rica soon. And we're gearing up to start another album so… things are going to change."

"Yeah," I agree, my chest tightening at the mention of The Burnt Clovers.

I feel my brother's eyes on my profile, studying me. "You hear from him?"

"Yes. We're emailing." I accelerate onto the highway. "You?"

"Just about band stuff."

I nod, not saying anything else.

"He doesn't call you?" Levi wonders.

I snort. "He calls me all the damn time. It's just…hard, to hear his voice."

Levi watches me closely. "Mav said he's struggling," he admits in a hushed tone.

"I'm trying to be there for him. As a friend, or whatever. But I need to protect myself too, you know?" I glance at Levi.

"Yeah. He's lucky to have you." It's strange because I know Levi is livid with Derek. They never had a chance to clear the air. Still, he wants good things for him. I guess he wants good things for me too.

I sigh. But what's good for Derek and what's best for me clearly aren't the same thing.

"You okay?" Levi asks after a few minutes of silence.

I glance at him and snort. "I should be asking you that."

He grins. "I'm better now that I'm with you. I'm looking forward to bunking together, Allegra. Reconnecting."

"Yeah, me too," I say, meaning it.

Levi and I drive the rest of the way home catching up and reminiscing. We talk about our childhood. About our family and our parents. About Boston and rehab and Derek and the band. About my friends and UCLA and the home-lessness outreach I've been doing.

Our chatter is incessant, like old times, and before I know it, I'm pulling into the parking spot outside my apartment.

"Nice place." Levi whistles.

A pang cuts through my chest. Weeks ago, I wondered what it would be like if Derek and I were a real couple, getting our first apartment together. Now, he's gone. And as much as I understand it, it still hurts. "Derek arranged it."

My brother looks at me, but I don't meet his eyes. "I'll take care of it," he says, with no judgement or frustration in his tone.

I dip my chin, nodding. I'd love to *not* owe Derek anything, and for that reason alone, I'll let my brother pay him back for the rent.

"Come on," I say.

Levi grabs his suitcase and together, we enter my home. Since it's a one-bedroom, he'll be crashing on the couch until we get a bigger place. Neither of us minds. It's an opportunity to reconnect. I've been waiting for it for years and this time, I think Levi has too.

"I'm going to call Jameson," Levi says, shaking his phone at me.

"Take your time. I'm going to take a quick shower," I say, yawning. I've been exhausted this past week. Maybe my late nights at Beirut are finally catching up to me?

Entering the bathroom, I flip on the shower. When I move to grab a towel from the linen closet, a box of tampons catches my eye and I freeze.

Staring at the box, I try to calculate my last period.

Shit. When was it?

I freeze, trying to recall a date but none come to mind. I can't remember when I last had it.

It must be stress. It has to be stress.

Still, when I spot the pregnancy test Nova left after she had a pregnancy scare, I swipe it and stare at the box.

There's no way I'm pregnant.

But taking the test can't hurt.

It will give me peace of mind.

Levi's voice mixes with the sound of the running water.

I sit down on the toilet and pee on the stick.

Then, I place it face up on the vanity and throw myself underneath the hot stream of water.

I'm fine. Everything is fine. I'm not pregnant.

The words play on a loop as I wash my hair and body. Heaving out a deep breath, I turn off the shower and wrap myself in a fluffy towel.

When I step out of the shower, I move toward the vanity.

I'm not pregnant.

I look at the test.

A positive fucking plus sign greets me.

Shock rocks through my nervous system and my limbs lock down.

I work a swallow and reach for the test with trembling fingers. Picking it up, I study the positive symbol. I hold the test at different angles in the light, making sure the light isn't playing tricks on my mind.

Nope. It's definitely positive.

Shit. My mind whirls and I plop down on the closed toilet seat, gripping the pregnancy test. My towel slides down one side of my body.

I'm having a baby with a rockstar.

A rock god who's currently reeling from discovering the identity of his biological father.

Bending over, laughter bubbles up and explodes from my mouth.

I'm having Derek "Reign" Reiner's baby.

And he has no fucking clue.

THANK you so so much for reading Resentful Rockstar! I hope you're loving Derek and Allegra's epic and emotional journey. Their story concludes in *Restless Rockstar,* out now!

The Score Keeper

Second Chance Chicago Series:

Broken Lies

Twisted Truths

Saving My Soul

Healing My Heart

The Kane Brothers Series:

Rescuing Broken (Jax's Story)

Recovering Beauty (Carter's Story)

Reclaiming Brave (Denver's Story)

My Christmas Wish

(A Kane Family Christmas

+ *One Last Chance* FREE prequel)

Finding Love in Scotland Series:

My Christmas Wish

(A Kane Family Christmas

+ *One Last Chance* FREE prequel)

One Last Chance (Daisy and Finn)

This Time Around (Aaron and Everly)

One Great Love

The College Pact Series:

The Last First Game (Lila's Story)

Kiss Me Goodnight in Rome (Mia's Story)

All the While (Maura's Story)

Me + You (Emma's Story)

Standalone

Corner of Ocean and Bay

ACKNOWLEDGMENTS

All my love and gratitude to Amy Parsons, Becca Mysoor, Erica Russikoff, Virginia Carey, Melissa Panio-Peterson, Sheila Dohmann, Dani Sanchez, Kate Farlow at Y'all. That Graphic, Rachel Lynn, and Amber for their support and friendship as I immersed myself in Derek and Allegra's journey!

A massive thank you and many hugs to the book bloggers, bookstagrammers, booktokkers, and book lovers for shouting out this trilogy and showing my characters so much love! Your support means the world to me.

To my family, love you the most. Thanks for encouraging me to chase my dreams.

ABOUT THE AUTHOR

Gina Azzi writes Contemporary and Sports Romance with relatable, genuine characters experiencing real life, love, friendships, and challenges. Dive into her hockey romance series: Ottawa Huskies, Boston Hawks, and Tennessee Thunderbolts or get lost in her rockstar romances in The Burnt Clovers trilogy.

A Jersey girl at heart, Gina has spent her twenties traveling the world, living and working abroad, before settling down in Ontario, Canada with her husband and three children. She's a voracious reader, daydreamer, and coffee enthusiast who loves meeting new people.

Connect with her on social media or through www.ginaazzi.com.

www.ingramcontent.com/pod-product-compliance
Lightning Source LLC
Chambersburg PA
CBHW030752190726
48285CB00003B/819